THAT NIGHT IN NASHVILLE

SAVANNAH KADE

1

Hailey Watkins had been having the time of her life when she saw *him*.

Her whole body froze and flash-heated at the same time. Her eyes went wide, and the world narrowed down to the cut of his shoulders, the color of his hair, the feelings that surged through her. She might just hyperventilate.

Maybe it wasn't him. She told herself it wasn't, that it couldn't be.

In her memory he was still sitting on the edge of her bed, in that little trailer in Carroll Hollow. Neither of them had enough money to even get to Knoxville.

She hadn't thought she'd ever see him again. Certainly not here in Nashville and certainly not in that suit, looking like the man she'd always known he'd grow into.

What would he even be doing at the festival anyway?

At first, she'd caught sight of the back of him and her heart had stuttered. Hard. Her brain had quickly shut that down. It didn't make sense that Adam would be here, so clearly it couldn't be him.

She'd climbed onto the temporary stage assembled for the

Nashville Brewer's Festival, her boots treading on the hot black surface. The squares were joined together and felt sturdy enough right now, but tomorrow? If the band started jumping? It would yield and sway a bit under her feet. She'd learned to roll with it and just keep singing.

Her label, Heart Beats, had her running around and singing every joint and fest they could get her booked at. It was hot, sweaty work for crowds who mostly hadn't heard of her. Hailey figured it was paying her dues, and she was willing to pay them. What most people hadn't figured out was that her tour bus—the one without her picture or name on the side, not yet—was nicer than the trailer she'd grown up in. The singing gig paid her actual money, and though it wasn't much, it beat working in the local factory.

Adam had gone to work in the factory. That's what he'd told her he was going to do, not that she'd stuck around to see.

The night she'd walked away, he'd yelled at her to *just go and leave it all behind*, including him. She'd been so hurt and so mad, that was exactly what she'd done. Now, with his words ringing in her head again, she put her vocal chords on auto pilot and kept singing even though no one was really listening except her sound guy.

He wasn't even *her* sound guy—Chad was there for all the performers. She was just the singer for the fifth slot as the festival changed from afternoon to night the next day. She hoped the attendees would have enough beer in them to give an unknown girl from outside Knoxville a chance—though she was hardly a girl anymore.

She'd been at this for eight years, waiting tables, performing at every open mic night, and opening for friends at clubs every chance she got. Now, she had the act down. Timing her breathing and watching where she planted her feet, Hailey sucked in a breath and went up for one of her high notes. She held it and fought a smile as a few of the workers stopped to listen and watch. She could do this.

Then the man in the suit turned around and the note cut off abruptly.

It *was* Adam.

The look on his face, though kind and clearly in charge, told her he'd been expecting to see her.

It wasn't fair. If he was here in a suit, then he would have seen the program. He would have seen her name in that fifth time slot, the one between the bigger acts than she.

Clearly, he'd had time to prepare for this non-reunion. She'd been blindsided by old memories running wild at just the thought that it might be him. Now, she was smacked again by grief, the kind she'd felt the whole first year she'd been gone. Hit by the feeling of the air being different just because he was close by—that feeling apparently hadn't gone away though she'd believed she was over him.

Nope. She wasn't.

She'd been so wrong about him.

He wasn't in the factory. He wasn't in Carroll Hollow. He wasn't stuck in the back hills of Tennessee, never having gone any further. He was here, in a damn suit that looked far too good.

The clothing was clearly tailored to fit him. It fit the new version of the man. He'd been just a boy when she left, when he refused to come with her. Clearly, everything was different for him now. Her, too.

She was standing on stage, doing lighting checks on her slinky top and swishy skirt and cowboy boots for tomorrow's show. She was doing sound check, so her high notes carried to the back of the crowd tomorrow. She'd come a long, long way. So she forced a smile onto her face, the same kind she used on stage, the one her manager called the "Megawatt Hailey." Pushing the grin up into her eyes and creating an expression she didn't feel, she made eye contact and gushed, "Adam!"

2

"Hey, Hailey!" Adam smiled around the name that used to roll off his tongue like honey and the promise of a future.

Thank God, he'd seen her name in the listings yesterday and stood stock still, the proverbial deer in headlights then, rather than now. Even so, he was confident he was staring at this blast from his past, despite the fact that he'd had time to practice smiling as though he was happy to see an old friend.

He was grateful now that he saw her for the first time while she was standing on stage, singing her heart out the same way she used to. Only, in the past, the stage had been in a high school auditorium. Her audience had been captive fellow classmates.

Now, she'd cut an album. She had an agent and she was on stage in a public place and getting paid to sing. She was no longer just a girl with dreams; she was a woman with a plan and a contract.

Adam turned his attention back to his work but there was no way to tune out the voice he once knew so well. She hit a high note, one that instantly took him back to her room. He'd sit cross legged on her bed while she would play her guitar and sing to him. Hailey would lean against a pillow shoved into the space where the bed was pushed against the wall—there was no headboard. Not in the tiny trailer with flimsy walls and flimsier doors. Surely the whole trailer park had heard her, but the sound was gorgeous.

As he looked up at the trusses and examined the projectors and rigging his workers had spent the morning assembling and checking, he could still hear her telling him all her plans. He remembered agreeing.

"One of the projectors went down, Boss." Tommy's voice interrupted his flashback.

Probably a good thing, Adam thought. He needed the distraction.

"Which one?" he asked as he followed his youngest tech across the open lawn to where the scaffolding was constructed at the back. Adam listened while the man explained that he wanted to replace the unit.

"Cables? Lens? Bulb?" Adam went down the checklist, unsurprised as Tommy nodded that he'd checked each of these already. Tommy was a high school dropout, but dedicated and smart. The only thing Adam had on Tommy was a diploma—not worth much—and a few years. Tommy could go far in the business. "You're right. It sounds like the motherboard. Well, better today than tomorrow."

Adam hopped on his phone, calling for a backup. Tommy didn't need instructions, just the go ahead. Adam gave him a thumbs-up before even hanging up the call. "It's on the way. Take care of it."

"Sure thing, Boss."

The "Boss" part was relatively new, and Adam had not yet grown tired of it.

Once it was confirmed the backup projector was on the way from the shop and Tommy was all set to install it, Adam looked up to the stage. Hailey no longer stood in the center under the spotlight. In her place stood four young men, guitars and basses haphazardly slung across their shoulders. One looked a little more cocky than the rest and he stood toward the front, hands clasped around the mic stand as though he were already singing.

Flipping through his paperwork, Adam saw that the group up after Hailey was a band called *Wilder*. They were also with Heart Beats, the production company that filled most of the afternoon gigs. Unable to help himself, Adam turned and examined the lead singer from the back of the lawn.

He had a megawatt smile and an *I'm-here-for-the-ladies* attitude. They hadn't yet started singing and it appeared someone had called Hailey back out on stage for a moment. She shielded her eyes and talked to the sound guy before turning back to the singer.

This time her smile wasn't the stage one. It was *real*. Her hand arched out and rested against the singer's bicep for a moment.

The twist of betrayal was sharp and sudden as he wondered if Hailey had gotten involved with this guy. But that wasn't right. He shouldn't feel anything, it wasn't his business whether she had or hadn't. There was no betrayal when they'd broken up years ago.

Once again, Adam forced himself to turn back to the task at hand. He'd just bought this company outright and he had to keep it profitable. He'd expected the stress, he just hadn't expected his own self-pressure to be quite as high as it was. Adam admitted to himself—probably for the fiftieth time—that he had something to prove, even if no one was paying any attention except him.

When the original owner started talking about retirement, he'd said he wanted to sell it to someone he trusted. That had been three years ago. Adam had made sure he became someone Clayton trusted. He and the old man had grown close and Adam had been the natural choice when Clayton finally retired and sold the shop last year. Adam now owned the company, and with it the title, the job, and the debt of the buy-out.

Even though Clayton Images and Sound was now his, everyone knew this was Clayton's company. So despite the fact that he'd bought the name and the building, he still had to prove himself.

Adam managed to keep his head in the game for one song, but when the band on stage opened up their second number—something about makeup sex, going to bed mad and all that—he gave up.

Turning and looking up the truss to where Tommy now perched at the top, Adam rattled off a handful of instructions and then acted as though there was something he needed to do. There *was*, it just wasn't work related.

He headed around the side of the venue where he'd seen Hailey disappear a handful of minutes before.

3

"**A**m I good?" Holding her hand up to shield her eyes from the summer glare, Hailey had looked around for her manager.

Hailey had been expecting Brenda, the woman who signed her, to be here. Instead, she found Ginger. It made sense, Brenda was a co-owner, she would likely not be out at the sound check for the Brewery Fest even if she did live in town.

"You're good to go!" Ginger gave her a thumbs up that passed blink-and-you-miss-it speed. Ginger was usually friendly, she was someone Hailey would call a friend outside of work, but during work? Both women weren't friends. They were here to get a job done.

Someone had tapped Ginger on the shoulder and the stage manager's attention had necessarily turned. Which was a shame, Hailey needed a friend far more than she needed a manager right now. But Ginger was gone, off in a zip, and Hailey was still alone with no one to tell that her stomach was in knots and the man at the back of the crowd was the one she'd once thought she'd spend her life with.

Faking nonchalance, Hailey waved to the stagehands around

her and headed toward the back, trying to ignore Adam the way he'd so easily ignored her. His back had been turned since their initial surprise at seeing each other and they'd both gone about their separate business.

Across another expanse of well-tended green grass, Hailey headed to a string of white tents fully covered by tough plastic "canvas." This was supposedly "backstage" where none existed. These fests were starting to get to her.

Her boots squished in the overly watered grass, heels sinking a little as she passed through the tent flap. A bead of sweat rolled down her back and she felt her shoulders hitch in an involuntary cringe. Sweating was fine, *if* she was doing something sweaty—say, hiking on a hot day, running, or having sex. This was not supposed to be sweaty—it was just sound check—and yet here she was, out in the sun and the heat. What was she even going to do tomorrow when she was on stage, singing her heart out, and sweltering in the late afternoon Nashville sun?

"Pay your dues, girl," she reminded herself under her breath as she slipped through another tent flap that separated several small areas designated as "dressing rooms." Names had been printed out on regular printer paper and stuck into place with gaffing tape by some assistant. *Not very Classy*. But she wasn't at "classy" yet.

Hailey finally found the small sectioned off area of the tent that bore a piece of printer paper with her name on it and suppressed a grin. It might be a crappy printout, poorly taped up, but it meant she was a *performer* at the fest, and meant she was getting paid, and that she got to hold center stage for a short piece of the afternoon.

Brenda's instructions about tomorrow had been clear. "Smile big. Win them over. Sell as many CDs, downloads, and auto-graphed posters afterwards as you can. Make them fall in love with you."

Simple enough. Though her thoughts were sarcastic, she'd do her best.

Slipping through the tent flaps into her own personal space, Hailey reached over and turned on the mega-size fan that had been set in the corner. It only took a few moments to realize it did nothing but blow the hot air around, but at least it felt marginally better.

Note to self, she thought *Walk into the venue tomorrow ready to go. Hair, makeup, probably even clothing—and only come in here after the show.*

As a mid-afternoon performer, it wasn't going to be any cooler tomorrow. Despite the heat and the non-ideal location for changing, she needed to get out of this outfit right away. She would need to wear it all again tomorrow. Her friend Shay Leland was hand-sewing everything Hailey wore on stage, and Hailey was not going to ruin it.

She still wasn't paying Shay what she was worth. But their friendship went back to elementary school and they were both working on moving up, each helping the other where she could. The band on stage after her—Wilder—was also wearing Shay's creations. She'd tailored four sleek, matching vests that looked like a cross between a bridal party and a wild country band. Coppery silk ties gave them an air of class and maybe even a little bit of punk irreverence. Yeah, Shay knew what she was doing, and Hailey would not ruin Shay's hard work, so she rapidly began unbuttoning the slinky shirt.

She'd carefully hang up the outfit that said, *Yes, I'm country, but not so country that you can't play me on the big radio stations.*

Someday.

Hailey was tucking that thought away for later as she heard a rustle behind her. She blinked and thought, *Strange.* Wasn't she the only one in the whole tent right now?

Here she was with her shirt half off. Not very professional. Pulling the fabric back together and clutching it in one hand, she turned around to be surprised all over again. She hadn't felt threatened at all—only concerned that someone was lost. But as she made eye contact, she realized he wasn't lost at all. He had come here specifically for her.

Adam.

4

"Hailey."

He whispered it and she caught the notes in his voice. She'd always loved that sound, but what she could never get a handle on was how he could make her melt with only her own name.

He'd ditched the suit jacket and rolled up his sleeves, something about the gesture more intimate than it should be. She was opening her mouth to ask him...what? *Anything*. Why he was here...in this tent? In Nashville? Or *Everything*. Why hadn't he come away with her? Had a minimum wage job at the factory and a mother who leaned too hard on him been a better choice than being with her?

None of those thoughts made it past her throat. What she said instead was just, "Adam."

She breathed it out like a one-word song, or maybe it was a prayer.

When she got lonely, she thought about Adam. When she broke up with yet another man who wasn't really a man, she thought about Adam. When she went home after a concert and didn't even have a cat, she thought about what it might be like if he'd been there waiting for her. They'd all been little prayers, she realized it now.

Still clutching at the front of her shirt, she waited for him to say more, but he didn't. He couldn't. His mouth was already touching hers. Soft lips seeking and needing.

Had he moved first? Or had she? She didn't know. It didn't matter as her eyes drifted shut and her body arched up into him. This was comfort. This was home. This was the man who turned her inside out, the only one who ever had.

Her blood rushed in her system and her arms snaked around his neck. Her shirt fell open, but she told herself it didn't matter...or maybe she just didn't care.

Adam stole her breath and gave her a rush all in the same move. Her lips parted under the onslaught and she felt his tongue searching for more than just her mouth. She'd give it. Anything. She'd always been a sucker for this man...even before he'd been a man.

This Adam was taller than she remembered, his shoulders broader, his physique more defined. Moving her hands outward, she felt the fine fabric of the white shirt he was wearing, but it didn't give way.

He was kissing her jawline and she was tipping her head back, her breasts on display in the nice bra she'd mistakenly worn. It was too hot for this bra today, but Adam was too hot for anything less.

"Jesus, Hailey."

Her belly clenched at the sound and her fingers went back to work. Tie. Already loose. She tugged at it then let it slip from her fingers to the grass below. Buttons. One undone. Two. Three...all the way down. This time as she pushed on the fabric it slid off his shoulders down to where it caught around his elbows. Somehow this was even sexier.

Tipping her head up as his mouth closed over the tip of her breast through the bra, she gasped and tugged his undershirt up.

Pressing her legs tightly together to quench the feelings Adam always stirred up, she found she was only winding herself up.

"Adam." She breathed his name again—a sigh, a wish, a need.

He answered by pushing her against the small, sturdy table that had been set out for her to use. Well, hell, she was going to use it.

His hands grasped her hips, and in a moment she was sitting on the edge, her legs wrapped around him as they continued to move against each other. She hooked her ankles together to keep him from getting away, though it was clear neither of them was going anywhere.

When his hand pressed against her back, she arched up, letting his mouth wander her breasts again. Only, at some time, he'd pulled the straps off her shoulders and she was exposed now. The feeling of his mouth on her transported her...she was in high school again. Learning about what felt good. Adam had taught her. Then she was back here. Right now. Hailey Watkins, singing at the Nashville Brewers Fest and apparently about to do her ex on her dressing room table. The very idea made her ache even more pronounced and she probably moaned.

Her fingers searched of their own accord. His pants were still on. She fumbled with his belt, finally pulling it free and dropping it into the grass on the growing pile of clothing. His hands were on her thighs, reaching up under her skirt, pushing it higher... higher. She opened the zipper of his pants, tugged at the elastic and cotton of his boxers and pushed downward.

He hissed in a breath as her fingers curled around the length of him.

"Hailey...Hailey..." He was panting then so she stroked him, and she felt the change as he lost control.

She would have smiled but he'd grabbed at her underwear and yanked it down her legs before she could grin, he'd gripped her hips and tugged her to the edge of the table even as her arms came up around his neck. She was kissing him with everything she was worth when she felt him push inside her. Her head tipped back and her lips let out an audible sigh at the familiar and still stunning feel of him.

Moving her hips, she took him deeper. She arched her back and gave in to the best sex she'd had in forever. Gave in to the feelings of safety and need and desire, a combination she couldn't remember ever having. She could feel a release building inside her. Fast and hard, it tore the fabric of the universe apart for a moment.

She only knew she didn't scream out and alert everyone beyond the tent because he was kissing her the whole time.

5

_____

Adam took a deep breath as he stepped back. It was the first moment since he'd seen Hailey that he was thinking instead of just feeling.

The high-powered fan humming loudly in the corner of the room blew at the loose sides of his shirt and reminded him he was standing there half naked. His button-down shirt hanging open, his undershirt rucked up into his armpits. His fly open. His pants down.

Jesus. He was a mess.

"Hailey?" This time he said it with all the confusion he had in him.

He must have said her name a hundred times in the past thirty minutes. Each time it had been said on a moan or growl or with the conviction of faith. This time, he didn't know what it meant.

On top of his own question, she asked, "What was that?"

He wanted to say, *I don't know,* but her name was the only thing that seemed to naturally roll off of his tongue. He couldn't find any words. So he shrugged, offering the only thing he had: doubt and more questions.

This time he watched as her eyes narrowed, clouded, and her head tipped.

She wasn't angry.

She was trying to figure out what the hell had just happened. The same as he was.

He knew that expression. He hadn't seen it in years, but he remembered it. He remembered *her*. Despite whatever trouble they'd gotten themselves into here, he suddenly saw that Hailey Pulaski was still in there. Even if no one knew that was her real name, he did. Adam remembered that her grandma had been a Watkins, and that she decided on this name for her career long before she'd finished high school. Long before she'd left town. He'd once told her he liked it. That "Watkins" was a good American name for a country singer. Salt of the earth and all that. "Hailey" gave her a more modern sound without being overly trendy.

It almost made him smile to think that she was Hailey Watkins because of what he'd said back then. But there was no time to stop and muse about what had been. They were standing in a tent, no real walls—only tent flaps—between them and the festival preparations outside.

Catching himself, he began to move. Adam's fingers flew rapidly, putting his clothing back to rights. Apparently, his movement was a signal that they were done here. Hailey began pushing her skirt around, twisting it and tugging at the zipper in the back that he hadn't bothered with. She'd already had her shirt half off when he'd walked in.

Maybe—just maybe—he could blame this whole episode on that. For a few minutes, they both worked in silence. Adam trying to make himself look as though the boss *hadn't* just stepped away for a quickie in a hot tent. And her completely changing clothes, brushing her hair out, and running a wipe over her face.

Without all the makeup, with her hair now slung up into a simple ponytail, she didn't even look like the same woman who'd walked in here. Even though he knew that both those women looked like his Hailey. It seemed she was also a professional at getting dressed. Despite having done twice the work he did, she was finished faster. So she squared up to him, crossed her arms and stared him down.

"I have to…I need…I—"

That stuttering way she cut herself off when she was flustered —he remembered that, too. It was cute. It tugged at his heart even when it shouldn't. This was the girl who'd *left him* when he needed her most. He tried to drill that into his brain because the rest of him wasn't really listening.

"I have some things to do to get ready for tomorrow." This time, all the words came out in one strong phrase and she didn't falter at all.

Adam could only nod and watch as she brushed past him, putting herself closer to the tent flaps. He thought she'd walk right out on those words, almost the way she had before. But, at the last moment, she turned.

"Maybe you should wait a few moments before you walk out."

The words cut him deep as she left.

Leaning back onto the table, as though she'd physically pushed him, Adam sat and stared at the tent flap as it fell back into place. Somehow, despite the fact that they'd been together for twenty minutes this time—instead of years—it felt as though she was leaving him all over again.

Last time, they'd talked about everything. They'd argued and yelled, and each had tried to cajole or even bribe the other into changing their mind. Neither of them had budged and that had been the end of it. He'd seen it coming then.

This time…they hadn't talked at all. But Hailey was just as gone as she'd been before. All he was left with was the soft sound of her footsteps in the too-wet grass.

Alone in the tent, he felt his heart let go of the feeling he'd been stabbed; now it sank. What had this interlude with Hailey been worth? Had he gotten anything out of it or had it only cost him?

He'd gone eight years without her. He'd gotten up every morning, did what he needed to do, and followed his own path. Adam had spent the intervening years learning not to hate her for leaving, even as he loved her more than anything. He reminded himself that Hailey had known about his mother and she'd *chosen* not to wait for him. In fact, she told him to leave his family and come with her.

Now, looking back, he could see that he'd made the right decision. This woman was harder and more determined than the soft, sweet Hailey he remembered. Had life made her that way or had she always been like this and he hadn't seen it? She'd sure had the strength to walk out the door and leave him behind years ago.

But maybe now he could see that she'd made the right decision.

The problem was that he'd believed he'd gotten over her. It was what he told himself on a daily basis. Seeing her again—*being with her again*—was now making him question all of it.

6

Hailey fought through the sensation that she was going to hyperventilate. *What had she done?*

There was no real answer other than she'd seen Adam and fallen right back into his arms and his bed. Or the dressing room table. Then she'd bolted without saying anything. Did he understand that every word clogged in her throat? She hadn't meant to be a bitch, she'd simply been too stunned to do anything other than run.

Pushing the thoughts aside as best she could, she drove into East Nashville, listening to her car as it rattled and wheezed. These were the normal rattles and wheezes—ones that she knew. Nothing to get worried about.

She hadn't ever owned a car that didn't make her neighbors raise an eyebrow or two. Every mechanic or hobbyist told her to get it looked at, but she wouldn't know what to do with a car that ran as smooth as butter or as quiet as a humming mouse.

She took a turn onto Marina Street. East Nashville was up and coming. her apartment building was not. She'd searched the listings for the cheapest place she could find. It had too many roaches. In the end, she'd sucked it up and paid a higher price for a buzzer at the door and a fourth-floor unit. It still wasn't even mid-range nice.

The building hadn't been updated since maybe the eighties. It needed a good pressure wash all over the outside if not new paint, but the owner wasn't going to do it. The landscaping had long since run wild. On one side of the long squat building, a set of shiny new condos had sprung up. Several lots down on the other side still had the older houses, but the fourth lot had been sold off. The lots were getting chopped in half and now sported duos of narrow, tall houses on thin slices of Nashville real estate. It was almost as if she could see gentrification creeping up to her door.

One of these days, everyone in the building would get a notice that the place had been sold. The neighbors bitched about it. The residents complained that the price had gone up. They complained that the building wasn't cleaned and the entry gate never got fixed. They cared; Hailey didn't.

As shabby as this was, she had come from far less. As much as they complained that they couldn't pay their bills, she knew how to survive on next to nothing. She didn't have a TV and therefore didn't have a cable bill. Her car rattled and wheezed, though it was paid off. She did have concerns about getting hit with repairs, but she'd reached an income level where she could generally make them as needed. That was a huge coup for a girl who'd grown up poor, constantly afraid that a tornado would whisk her trailer off to Oz—and not in a good way.

Parking under her designated section of sagging carport, she locked the car and climbed her three flights of stairs. There was no elevator here. And no front gate. She locked everything. After undoing the three locks on her door with three separate keys, Hailey turned around and slid the bolt behind her.

It was only then that she let herself admit what she had done. Sinking back against the door, suddenly she felt like she was in the past again, with Adam. It wasn't the interlude in the tent that washed over all her senses, it was years of history. If she let her eyes close, she could almost smell the fried food from the trailer next door.

Her best friend Shay and her little sister Zoe had been raised on chicken fingers, cheese sticks, and apple pies. Mrs. Leland had gotten a deep fryer from some boyfriend or other and she'd cherished the thing. The entire trailer smelled of fryer grease until long after Shay and Zoe moved out, Hailey was sure. That fryer had been the prize of the little gravel street for a while. Even Hailey saved her pennies to buy pies to put into it.

For all the Lelands had only the fryer as anything decent, her own family had been no better off. The kids had shared, sneaking each other food when one family had lean times. But there were months when both families had been reduced to beans and oatmeal and no one had a decent snack in sight.

Adam's family wasn't much better off than the families in the trailer park. Though still from the wrong side of town and too close to the trailers to be classy, Adam's family had at least owned a house. No matter how falling-down it was, it was still its own structure and therefore a level above anything Hailey's mother had managed to achieve.

The memories washed over her: sitting on his bed, doing their homework together, and eating after-school snacks. Mrs. Zucker worked but she insisted that there was something in the house like carrot sticks or bananas for Adam and his younger sisters. Sometimes Hailey even deigned to eat one. It was more care than her own mother managed. Mrs. Zucker wasn't home, and she was manipulative and forceful with her kids, but at least she cared. It was more than Hailey could say for her own mother.

Her thoughts shifted of their own accord. Though she knew she was still leaning against the door in her own apartment, that she'd paid for with her own money, that she'd earned by singing, mentally, she was back at Adam's house. Angry, frustrated, and hurt.

On that last day, she'd stood at the foot of the bed, hands clenched into fists, and she'd yelled at him. "We were supposed to leave together!"

"My mother found a lump. I have to stay. You know my dad can't deal with this!" He'd begged her to wait.

"Your mother is milking this! It's probably nothing!"

Thinking back, it sounded cruel. His mother might have cancer and she'd told him to leave home anyway. But it was well within Mrs. Zucker's range to pull something like this. She'd made it clear more than once that Hailey was a "silly girl with stupid dreams." His mother had told her she'd most likely wind up a whore sleeping on the streets. She'd made it clear, in no uncertain terms, that he was throwing his life away if he went with Hailey...and Mrs. Zucker wasn't going to let her only son throw his life away.

Of course, she'd pull something like suddenly having cancer under some seriously suspicious timing.

So Hailey had begged him to leave. He'd begged her to stay. In the end, she left and he stayed and they'd both been angry and hurt.

Adam Zucker was going to stay in Carroll Hollow and take a job in the chicken factory at the edge of town. In fact, Shay had told her once that's exactly what he did. So why was he here now? Why was he in Nashville, in a suit, setting up lights and projectors for her show?

She was supposed to have left him and the trailer in the tiny town outside of Clinton in her rearview mirror. But now, here he was, and Lord what they'd done.

She hadn't asked about his mom or the chicken factory or even whether or not he still lived in Carroll Hollow. Even though she'd managed to duck out today—hopefully with some of her dignity still intact—she was going to have to see him again tomorrow.

What was she going to do?

7

"So, you're playing the Brewers fest. Anything else lined up?" It was a dumb question. But it was all that Adam managed to make come out of his mouth. Simply being near Hailey short-circuited his brain.

Today, he'd caught her before she went on stage and asked if she'd meet him here after. He suggested they could catch up. He'd shamelessly played the "for old times' sakes" card.

But everything had been awkward today. Had he expected her to leap into his arms? No. Not after yesterday's "I have things to do" walkout. He should be at the fest right now, making sure all the equipment was working, that all his techs were where they were supposed to be, and that he was on hand to troubleshoot anything that went wrong. Instead, he'd put his project manager in charge and ignored the look he'd gotten from Tommy as he left for the bar he'd picked out for this meet-up with Hailey.

At first, he'd sat here, afraid she would stand him up. He'd ordered a beer and drunk the whole thing before deciding that was a piss poor plan. Then he'd switched to nervously snacking on chips and salsa while he waited. When she'd showed up, smiled and waved as she wound her way through the crowded space, he thought everything would be okay.

Instead, they sat across a large booth intended for far more than two people and stared at each other like strangers—well, strangers who'd screwed inside a tent at a brewery fest yesterday. Strangers with a past too complicated to untangle over a beer.

"I'm at The Bluebird on Tuesday," she offered up and he wanted to smile for her. The Bluebird had been on her list of goals, but she didn't stop to acknowledge either that she'd made it or that he knew she had. "After that, we're heading up into Kansas, Oklahoma, Illinois. A bunch of stops across the country."

"You're on tour?"

She nodded softly and sipped at the beer she'd ordered.

Something reached inside his chest, grabbed his heart and squeezed. She was already leaving, and he'd only just found her again.

But he hadn't found her. She wasn't his, despite yesterday afternoon's interlude. She clearly wasn't going to throw away her dreams and stay with him. She hadn't the first time, when she'd actually been his girlfriend, she surely wouldn't now.

Adam tried to focus on everything else. There was so much more to talk about. Even if they couldn't untangle the past, they had to untangle at least yesterday. But still, all he could think about was seeing her up there on that stage.

He hated that her dreams had taken her away from him. And he loved that she'd made it. Maybe she wasn't playing an arena yet. Maybe she was opening for a band who was opening for someone else who was opening for a headliner that was playing much later in the evening, but she was on stage.

The crowd had loved her today. He'd watched as she took the stage to a loosely populated lawn. People had come in with plates of food and steins of beer. More and more had sat down or stood and swayed despite the humidity and the direct sun. She'd charmed them all.

She even had paraphernalia to sign in a tent after her show. Adam had thought about getting one of the posters from her, but her handlers had lined people up to get her autograph. He wasn't about to stand in that line to get his signed merch and then get quickly shuffled out of the way so she could John Hancock the next one. He could see himself protesting, "No, man, I really do know her!" but what if Hailey didn't protest with him? What if she just smiled at him to scoot along and let her get to her next fan? He hadn't even tried it.

For years, he dreamed he would hear on the radio that she had a show in town. If the music industry ran on pure talent, Hailey would have already been a star. He thought maybe he'd buy a ticket when she came to town. In his daydreams, he might stand in line and wait, only to have her scream out his name and dive across the stage or the signing table to envelope him in a bear hug and say how much she missed him.

Clearly, that was not how their reunion had gone.

The silence settled in at the table and the nerves ran in small circles in his chest. Adam ran his hand down his new glass of beer, wiping the sweat onto the coaster. He watched as Hailey picked hers up, attempting to sip, but nervously gulping. Maybe that was what had made him start speaking—so she couldn't immediately start yelling at him.

She was swallowing when he said it. Bad timing on his part.

"We didn't use any protection yesterday."

Though she choked a little and coughed, she didn't get mad. He'd been expecting more. He'd had other girlfriends since Hailey, and he was used to being blamed for any errors.

She coughed again as she waved a hand at him. With a deep breath, she looked up at him as though he wasn't talking about them having sex in her dressing room tent yesterday. "Don't worry." Her words were steadier about this than about anything else she'd said since she arrived at the table. "The timing is all wrong. There's nothing to be concerned about."

"But I am concerned," he pressed, still confused by her lack of worry. Was she on the pill? Accidents happened. She didn't say anything, and he pushed. "You're leaving town in a bit—heading out all over the country. It's practically impossible for a woman to have a child she doesn't know about, but it's definitely something that can happen to a man."

He watched as her eyes slowly narrowed at him. This time they didn't gloss over. This time she didn't tip her head. He knew this expression, too. He'd stepped in it—big time.

8

Was he serious?

Hailey felt her blood start to boil, and all the beer in the world wouldn't have calmed her down. She tried to count to ten but barely made it to three before she blurted out, "Do you really think I would run off and have your child—on my *own*—and not tell you?"

As though her words pushed him physically, his head had slowly pulled back away from her. Obviously, he needed to say *no*. But also obviously, some part of him *had* thought it was possible.

Putting her hands flat on the table—she at least managed to refrain from actively slapping them down—she leaned forward. "Listen. I live in a small, one-bedroom apartment. There is no space for a baby. I'm going to be on the road for the better part of the next six months. Let's discuss what it looks like to have a pregnant country star up on stage. An *unmarried* one." She waited a beat while he managed to only raise one eyebrow while still looking contrite. "Yeah, it's not gonna fly. So maybe this little meeting is over, and you *don't* need to worry about it."

Her hands were still pressed flat against the tabletop. Pushing herself up awkwardly, she slid out of the booth and stalked toward the front door. *Let him pay for her beer*, she thought. She'd intended to cover herself. But now? No.

She felt his presence following along. Or she smelled the hint of his aftershave—the same one he'd worn when she'd been in high school. Or maybe she was just so in tune to him that she simply *knew* he was right behind her without looking. She was ready even before she felt his hand on her arm. So at least it didn't jerk her backwards, but it did stop her angry march out of the joint.

Still mad, she turned to face him. "What do you want? Do you have more ways to insult me, Adam?"

Shaking his head, he only said, "No." Then he immediately dialed back. "I'm sorry. I didn't intend to insult you in the first place. I just didn't want to lose an opportunity."

Her eyes narrowed at him, then she glanced down at his hand, still clasped around her forearm. She watched as he loosened his hold and his fingers slid downward toward her wrist. He was almost holding her hand.

"What kind of opportunity do you see here?" she asked, truly wanting to know.

"Come back to the table." He sighed it out. The words were a soft command but the emotion made it into more of a plea. It was getting to her; he always did. "Come back before the server clears our beer away. Let me buy you dinner. Let's just talk, just catch up for a moment."

But Hailey didn't move. His request sounded reasonable. Then again, saying hello to him yesterday had sounded reasonable too and look where that had gotten her! He tugged on her wrist once and she began to follow along, thinking through everything that had landed her in this position. Saying hello yesterday had gotten her into the tent. The interlude in the tent had gotten them here. At least this was a public restaurant and they couldn't do anything untoward on this table.

Not here. Not in the booth. But thinking that they couldn't do it on the restaurant table made her *imagine* it. Her mind flashed with images of him sweeping the beer onto the floor, unconcerned about the mess and the broken glass, only focused on her. She could see him laying her back onto the tabletop and...

She wanted to wonder where that had come from. But the fact was, she knew this was Adam. This was *her*. And had yesterday really been all that unexpected? He was the one man who'd ever made her want to throw everything away and just stay with him. She'd always wondered if she ever ran into Adam again would they get back together? Sleep together? Now she didn't have to wonder.

Her other thought—that she might see him and realize that she was finally, truly *over* him—had not happened. She wasn't over him. She could feel the heat from his touch all the way up her arm and she wanted to feel it everywhere else. Just like yesterday. Bad decision or not.

He guided her back into the seat at the booth, almost as though he wanted to be sure she was firmly in and wouldn't slip out and run away. The beer was still waiting for them—still cold, still sweating onto the coaster as though needing something to do. She picked it up and took another sip.

When the silence stretched between them and it became clear that he hadn't thought past getting her back into the booth with him, she asked, "What is it that you want to know?"

Adam looked like it pained him to ask. But he asked anyway. "When you left, where did you go?"

He didn't have to clarify. They both knew what it meant —*When she left.*

"I came to Nashville. Just like I said I would." The last phrase came out a bit defensive. She wished he hadn't said it, but he didn't seem to take it badly.

"So you've been here ever since?"

Hailey shook her head. "Nashville was hard at first. I cut a CD on my own, paid for it out of savings, knocked on doors to hand it to agents. But I was just another kid with a demo. I mean, they liked me, but there was always something that kept them from actually signing me."

"If you didn't stay here the whole time then where did you go?"

"Los Angeles." She said it with a grin and a tip of her beer as though toasting something imaginary.

"Was it better out there?"

She had to shrug at that. She was telling him the easy parts of her story. Not how she'd huddled on her cheap motel bed with the chair wedged under the flimsy doorknob, equally afraid of the predators she'd been warned about and looming failure. How should she say it? "There were more struggling artists in LA than in Nashville. I'd anticipated that the rent was higher, but I hadn't saved enough extra. Still, the weather was great and despite all the struggling artists, there weren't that many country singers. Waitressing jobs expected that you would have a script in your back pocket to wave at any influential patrons. So when I had sheet music, or a country music CD, it made me a little unique. I joined SAG—"

"The Screen Actors Guild?" he asked incredulously. "I didn't know you wanted to be an actress."

"I didn't. But it was pretty easy to get work as an extra. It paid well enough, and it allowed me a lot of open time."

"Were you in anything I might have seen?" Now he was grinning, and she could feel her face starting to widen into a smile as well. This was *her Adam*, the Adam who was happy for her. Who was proud of her achievements. The one she'd remembered from back before they started fighting.

She rattled off a few films she'd been an extra for and watched as his eyes widened. He could never hide anything from her, and she could tell right now that he'd seen her in the crowd scenes.

Up until this moment, he probably thought he'd imagined that it was her.

She understood. There'd been so many times walking down the street she would catch a glimpse of someone and think it was Adam. She would run a few steps to catch up, only to discover she'd been wrong.

"But you didn't stay in LA."

She shook her head. "Three years. Nothing panned out there either. I did a few gigs here and there, but didn't get an agent, and by the time three years was up, I'd gone to all of them. So I packed everything up and drove across the country again. When I came back to Nashville, things were better for me. I don't know if I was a more 'seasoned' performer or what. But I started playing clubs and earning some money. Then, almost a year ago, everything changed."

9

She'd done it, Adam thought.

Hailey had moved several times and it hadn't happened instantaneously, but she'd gotten signed to a record deal—if they still called them that. He'd seen the poster they put up for her. The advertising said *a voice like God's own hurricane*. They weren't wrong.

She wasn't waiting tables anymore or being an extra in crowd scenes. She was paying her bills by singing on stage. She had to be so proud. He knew because *he* was. Though it hadn't happened to him yet, he knew he would hear her song on his radio in the next few days. Adam knew his hand would change the station and wait to hear her now. So far, he'd simply been avoiding country music so he wouldn't hear her. That was hard to do in Tennessee, but he'd managed it.

As kids, they'd listened all the time. She loved it so much and he'd always known that one day he would hear her voice through the speakers. After she left, he'd known that hearing her on the radio would break his heart.

According to their original plans, he would have been there beside her, holding her hand, and listening to her scream with delight the first time her song aired. But that moment had passed without him.

He'd effectively avoided Hailey Pulaski/Watkins for eight long years. He'd made sure he didn't inadvertently hear her voice. He'd put away all the pictures he had of her. He'd even pushed her out of his thoughts. But now that they'd made love in her dressing room tent, things were different. Surely, he could change the radio station and handle what he heard.

One day, probably soon, she wouldn't just be a local country singer. She'd be big, a national star.

He was waiting for her to shift from telling him what she'd already done and start into her plans. Hailey always had plans. She had steps and a rundown. She understood things might not go in the order she thought, or that she might have to knock on more doors than she wanted, but she always had it all figured out. Maybe not a checklist hung on her wall, but certainly firmly in her head.

She surprised him by not saying any of that. "I thought you were going to go work in the chicken factory. How does that get you into Nashville, rigging a brewers festival country show...in a suit?"

He hadn't quite wanted to go into this. His plan had been to talk about *her*. If they talked about him, they'd eventually get to the part that made him hate her sometimes. So he glossed it over. "I *did* work at the chicken factory for two and a half years."

He watched as her eyebrows climbed. But instead of pushing harder, she took a sip of her beer. She did it sweetly, almost as though she were flirting with him. Though he held off saying more, she waited him out. She'd always had the ability to make him talk. "A family moved into the house next door to us and fixed it up. It turned out the father was a manager at a video equipment company. I hassled him for six months for a job here or there. So while I was still working at the factory, he managed to get me a couple of extra evening and weekend gigs, pushing around the crates. It wasn't great money, but it was *extra* money. And unlike the factory, I didn't have to wait until someone died or retired in order to move up."

He paused, but she still wasn't jumping into the space. "After a handful of months, they either decided I knew enough or that they were short-handed enough that I was allowed to help set up the staging. I got a slight pay raise and things went up from there. I made friends with the owner, got more jobs. Eventually it was enough work to quit the factory."

Adam smiled when he said it. He could feel the rush all over again. It had been a proud day. He'd handed in his two weeks notice because he didn't want to be the guy who just walked out. Those two weeks had been the hardest weeks of his work there, knowing he was free of the hated job. Almost.

He didn't tell Hailey any of that. He once again figured he'd let it drop there. But Hailey was still Hailey, and she pushed again. "So you decided to wear a suit when all the other guys are running around in their black cargo pants and black t shirts on a hot summer day? I don't think so. You've got more to explain."

He gave her the short version. "When the owner retired, I bought the company from him."

"You *own* it?" He watched as her mouth fell open. Eight years they'd been apart and still this moment was more than gratifying. Yes, he'd stayed in Carroll Hollow. Yes. He'd stayed in the dingy house for a long time. For years they'd barely had enough for basic repairs, let alone enough money to fix it up. And yes, he'd stayed out of a sense of obligation. But he hadn't stayed stagnant.

She may have gone out and made something of herself. He may have stayed put, but he'd made something of himself, nonetheless.

"Are you still in Carroll Hollow? I mean, are you traveling here for this job in Nashville?"

Adam shook his head. "My mom is still in the same house, but I'm not. Clayton Images and Audio has our office in Knoxville.

We work all over the area though." He didn't add that his dream was to open up a Nashville branch, then a third in Atlanta. But he wasn't there yet. He was still buried under mounds of debt from buying out Clayton. He didn't tell her that either. She wouldn't be around long enough for it to matter. He ignored the stabbing feeling in his chest and smiled. "I have an apartment in Knoxville."

Her head tipped in for a moment. He wondered if she was disappointed that he wasn't living here in Nashville. It was certainly something he'd considered.

Her head was tipping side to side as she considered all the things he'd told her. He didn't even know if she knew she did it, but it definitely meant she was thinking about something. He glanced down at his watch instead of looking at her more, and he didn't like what he saw.

"I've got to get back. I have to be there when the main shows go on." Adam felt bad as soon as the words were out of his mouth, as though he'd insulted her by stating she wasn't one of the biggest shows. But the timing said she wasn't.

"Of course," she agreed readily. "Shall I get the check?"

"No. I invited you, I'll pay." Raising his hand, he caught the server's attention, and the check was pulled out with disturbing efficiency. He'd been hoping to milk a few more minutes out of this. He handed over his credit card and only managed a few more trite statements before the card and his slip were back and his time was up.

They headed out the front door together. But once they were on the sidewalk, he and Hailey said goodbye and went different directions. Only then did he realize he hadn't asked if he could see her again.

He didn't know if he ever would.

10

Hailey headed straight home after the short prelude with Adam. She'd intended to stay at the festival and support the other artists on stage. She was great at standing in the audience and calling out and cheering these days. She could get a crowd going for a new artist, just pretending she was an enthusiastic listener—and she was.

But today she didn't have it in her. She'd known she wouldn't be able to watch the bands while she was there, she'd be too busy watching Adam run the show. She'd wanted to stay and catch *Wilder*—the group she was sharing her tour with. But they'd gone out directly after her, almost passing each other backstage and she'd been pulled aside into her signing booth.

Brenda had done a fantastic job with the PR. By the time Hailey arrived at the signing tent, a crowd waited for her. Hailey knew better than to believe it was all about her singing. It was marketing, and it was hustling, pure and simple—but she'd still had a tent with a crowd. That had felt good.

Once she'd been ousted for Wilder to take over the small booth, she'd been ready to meet up with Adam. But their conversation had worn her out—mentally, if not physically.

At home, she'd been almost too exhausted to plug her laptop into the monitor she'd bought secondhand and used as a TV screen. She'd been sluggish logging into her streaming services, but Hailey pep-talked herself into watching a few more episodes of a show she'd been bingeing until earlier this week. Maybe she could catch up a little bit.

She'd been asleep before she hit the third episode.

On Sunday, she'd gotten up and made herself coffee in the cheap coffee maker. Looking around at the small apartment, it was clear she was definitely a former poor kid. She had *things*. She didn't have quality items, she had lots of cheap items. A lot of it she'd gotten at Goodwill and just never replaced. The coffee pot might have been purchased new but, given the sputtering and whining noises it was making, she definitely hadn't gotten a quality item there.

Was her philosophical self-check brought on by seeing Adam again? Probably. But she didn't need a blast from her past. Aside from Adam and Shay, she'd been willing to walk away from all of it. She didn't even know if her own mother was still in the trailer park or if she'd moved or re-re-re-married or what. Hailey could only assume that Donna Pulaski wasn't dead or she would have heard about it.

She pushed any deep thoughts aside and slowly rolled into her day. Only she didn't roll, Hailey procrastinated. She messaged Shay and caught her at a good moment. On video chat with her best friend, she confessed to everything she'd done—much to Shay's surprise. Then she listened as Shay worried about her young sons, both of whom were out with their fathers for the weekend.

"They'll be okay," Hailey reassured her friend, though they both knew it wasn't anything she could promise.

Shay nodded as though trying to convince herself and changed the subject. "You'll have to keep me posted about Adam. I admit, I didn't see that coming!"

After she hung up, Hailey got dressed and finally got her ass out the door and down to Love Note's studios. Parking at the back, she headed inside and found more activity there.

There were a few dedicated songwriters like her in on a weekend day. JD Hewlitt occupied one of the back rooms. Through the tiny window in the door, she could see him with his headphones on, head down, moving with music no one else could hear as his fingers crawled agilely along his guitar strings.

She'd once considered getting involved with one of the Hewlitts—JD or his younger, bolder brother. TJ was a bit too wild for Hailey's tastes, and JD wasn't in any space for a relationship. His new daughter was already enough for him to handle, and besides, Hailey had met his neighbor Kelsey and it was pretty clear that JD had a thing for his neighbor. Hailey had liked Kelsey on the spot and she wasn't getting in the middle of that. Passing by without knocking she headed down the hallway.

Peeking through the window of the next closed door, she found Margaret, an older woman with an adorable silver ponytail, also with her head down over her work. Noise didn't leak in or out of the newly redesigned workshop rooms, so Margaret must have been paying attention and caught the movement at the door, unlike JD.

Looking up and smiling, the older woman waved, giving Hailey a warm fuzzy feeling that she needed this morning. Margaret and Hailey were slated to write a song together—something Brenda had decided would be a good idea. The label manager thought their styles matched. Margaret was definitely old school, but she was more than up to speed on what sold a song. Most people would have balked at writing country music with a woman in her sixties, but Hailey was excited and she waved back with a big grin on her face.

Today wasn't the day to start on whatever that piece would become though. Margaret was clearly neck deep in something of her own. So Hailey passed by looking for an empty room. There was something about having her guitar slung over her shoulder as she looked for a place to sit down and sing that made it feel like a throwback to before she had an album out. Before she had a contract. Before she'd been the one on the stage. Before she could pay her bills.

The room was definitely an upgrade from the horrible acoustics of her early apartments. It was an upgrade from the banging on the floor, a commentary from the people downstairs if they decided she played too late into the night. Hailey put her name on the board on the door, noting that it was already reserved at two. She'd probably be out of here before then anyway.

Stowing her things, she grabbed a cup of coffee from the break room because a second cup of coffee today would be fine. And probably so would a third, or a fourth... She needed it to do good work, and she needed good work to stay in the business. It was the lie she told herself to keep drinking the coffee.

At last, when she settled in, staff paper spread in front of her so she could record what she did, she turned on the built-in recording device in the corner of the room. It would collect not only her music, but her mutterings and the long spaces in between.

Picking up her guitar, she was pleased to find this was one of those mornings when a tune came out easily. She worked with it, building in her bridge. The chorus and verse parts came along with a little work and some vocal checking.

But the words were harder to get out.

Every time she started to sing, it was about Adam.

11

———

Hailey stood quietly, listening as her newest song played into the soft air of the office while Brenda sat behind her desk with absolutely no expression on her face. This was one of Brenda's best skills and probably why she was succeeding as a new label owner. She could listen to anything and formulate any reaction she chose. No one would know what her reaction was until she decided to share it.

Though Hailey hadn't used Adam's name, anyone in the know would recognize that it was a song about him. The idea had been inescapable for the last week and a half.

She'd been frantically writing new music. Songs about saying goodbye, songs about making hard choices, and even one about finding the one who got away. That one wasn't real. She wasn't kidding herself. She and Adam weren't picking up where they left off, but the song about it—about what might have been—it was good. She could only hope Brenda thought so, too.

As she watched her manager listen carefully, Hailey wondered how much of hers and Adam's story Brenda could glean from the song. Could she tell that Hailey and Adam were no grand love story? They'd simply run into each other after a long time, and they'd hooked up. That wasn't the song though. The song had bigger dreams. The song was great.

Or Hailey thought so. It took another full minute for Brenda to raise one eyebrow, before she said, "Wow."

Hailey let out all the breath she had been holding as she tried to get her own poker face to be anywhere near as good as Brenda's. It didn't work, so she just asked "Yes?"

"Oh, definitely." Leaning forward, Brenda tapped the end of her pen on the desktop as she clearly began thinking through the logistics. Once Brenda told you how she felt about your song, she would easily show every thought and feeling on her face. So it was easy for Hailey to read now that Brenda was making decisions.

Hailey, still standing, took in another deep breath and steeled herself for whatever her boss had to say. She still wasn't prepared.

"So we've hit a bit of a snag with the tour."

Oh? This was the first she was hearing of it.

Brenda went on. "One of the guys in Wilder inherited a five-year-old recently—"

"I'm sorry. *What?*" Hailey asked.

"It's his kid. But he didn't know he even had a child. The mother died and finding out he had a daughter was a shock."

"Wow, which one?" Hailey knew these guys, or she thought she did. She was shocked one of them might have a mysterious kid in the back corner.

Brenda stunned her further by saying the last name Hailey expected. "JD."

"Oh." She felt the word slide out of her mouth again. She'd known JD had a daughter but had no clue it was that crazy of a situation. Still, she struggled to figure out how this was her problem.

"So, they can't go out on tour full-time like I'd been planning for them. What I want to do is alternate their tour dates with yours."

Hailey felt her heart sink. She'd been told she would be on tour herself *full-time*. She had plans to put her things into storage and be on the road for almost six months, hitting every tiny fair and festival along the way. Apparently, JD and his crazy love child meant that now *Hailey* couldn't go. She tried to keep her smile in place, even though she was certain she was failing miserably.

"Alternating the dates still gives us one complete tour. It also gives you a chance to ease into your first tour rather than get slammed into it. Touring is hard. I like this solution. It allows JD time to be at home and to be a father." Brenda cut herself off and changed directions, apparently seeing the expression on Hailey's face. "Look, I'm here, rather than in LA or New York because family is the most important thing. You know this. Everyone here knows why we founded Heart Beats. I ran myself ragged and my husband raised my kids and I was pretty sure they didn't recognize me. So understand that I'm not going to do that that to him."

Hailey nodded trying to look for an upside to getting downsized. Brenda had seen right through her uncharitable and selfish feelings and Hailey wasn't sure if she'd just been chastised or not. But Brenda wasn't wrong. JD *did* need time, and family *was* important.

Still, Hailey had made her sacrifices. She'd walked away from everything to pursue this career and, as much as she agreed with Brenda, and as much as she understood JD needed time, it didn't seem fair to pull *her* because of *his* mistake.

But Brenda had said her piece and she was moving on to the next topic. Hailey scrambled to catch up.

"—and I want to pull your album."

"*Why?*" Could this day get any worse? First, she'd given Brenda a great song, but everything was getting taken away! Why would they pull her album? It hadn't even been released yet, so it couldn't have performed badly.

"I want to rework it." Brenda was tapping her pen on the tabletop again.

Hailey sat down abruptly in the chair across from Brenda's desk and clutched her hands in her lap. This was more than she'd bargained for and she wasn't fooling anyone about her growing distress, so she just let it all hang out. "I thought you liked the new song." She'd thought it might go on her third album. *Damn*. Maybe she wasn't going to get one. Maybe she was over before she'd even started.

The music industry was full of failure. She was about to be next and she was struggling both to breathe and to not burst into a fit of tears or anger.

But Brenda was shaking her head.

"No, it's not like that. See, I thought we were going to put your album out and that we would get some traction with it. We would use it to build your fan base more and then, with your third album, we could see a real hit. I thought it might happen then because some people would already know you and like your music."

Well that was good, but it didn't explain anything. Hailey clutched her hands harder and waited.

"I think you're fantastic." Brenda was leaning forward, but now she was no longer tapping the pen. She was making a point, and she needed Hailey to listen.

At least it became a little easier to breathe after hearing that. But only a little.

"What I thought," Brenda said, "was that we were going to *roll* you into things. I thought it would be a slow build. But after this song, I think we can do better than that. If you can give me a couple more like this, we're going to rework this new album. We're going to pull a few of the songs. I like them, but maybe we sell them to somebody else. You'll get songwriting credit, they can perform it, whatever, I don't know."

She took a deep breath and looked Hailey in the eyes. "If you can give me two or three more like *this one*, then we're going to drop this new album to the biggest splash Heart Beats has ever seen."

It was Hailey's turn to lean back. She was stunned. Could she do a few more of these? She didn't know. "I mean," her mouth opened, and she started talking without thinking first. "This is one of about four songs I wrote the other day."

"Why didn't you play them all for me?" Brenda frowned suddenly.

"Because honestly, they're all the same theme." Hailey could feel her eyes squinting, as though she were apologizing as she spoke.

Brenda nodded, "I get it."

Did she? Hailey thought. Then again. Brenda did live and work with songwriters. She probably knew when big things happened in her artists lives, because they tended to put it in a song.

"Give them to me. Let me listen and let's decide together." Brenda's demands felt better than her earlier explanations. Hailey was thinking through all the changes. Was she good with losing some of her tour dates? She was muddling it through when Brenda cut into her thoughts again. "Are you okay if I change some of them around?"

"I don't understand," Hailey asked before she even processed the question. The one thing she understood about Brenda was that Brenda was *not* a songwriter. Brenda was a great producer. She knew what she liked, knew what she heard and was able to look at an artist and say, *no, go higher, change the bridge, add a background chorus*. But Brenda didn't write music.

Then Hailey understood. "You want to tweak them?"

"Well, I want to see if there's something else we can use that we can tweak around to make into a separate song. Hailey, I can tell you bled for this song."

Hailey nodded, but Brenda wasn't done.

"But whatever you did, it was amazing. I'm going to need you to bleed for the next three, too."

12

Adam sat at his desk with his head in his hands.

"Hey boss!" Jerry had stuck his head in the door and waited until Adam lifted his eyes and actually looked at him.

Damn, Adam thought, even as he looked up, this wasn't going to be good. If it was just an update, his best friend would have barked it at him and been gone before Adam even had a chance to respond. "What is it?"

"We may have to turn down the Hilton job."

"Why?" The Hilton job was huge. Adam had been counting on it even though it wasn't fully confirmed yet. Adam knew better than to anticipate thing before they were signed. Even when contracts were all signed and the job was completed, he didn't count on anything until the paycheck was in his hand. But he *needed* the Hilton job. It was big enough to change the depth of the debt he was drowning in.

"We don't have all the equipment," Jerry said.

Adam felt his face pull into a frown wondering how ridiculous Jerry could get. "Then sub-rent it." It was the obvious solution. One they'd used on many, many occasions.

"I'm not finding it. Not on those dates." Jerry shrugged. "I've tried piecing it together from different places, but even that's not getting all that we need. I think we need to buy the equipment."

Oh, dear God, Alex thought. The last thing he needed was to go further in debt for this company. At the level of professional display and audio services his company offered, the equipment was worth millions. Sub-renting it dug into their profits, but buying it outright? That could eat everything. It would set them up well for the future, but only if they bought wisely.

He could not deal with this today, but he wasn't convinced that Jerry was wrong. The Hilton job would cover the extra equipment, as long as the job came through, and as long as they paid him on time.

"Look," Jerry said, "it's about having the amount of equipment when we need it. It's your company and your decision. But we should be able to send these projectors out in the future for good money. They're in relatively high demand, which is why I'm struggling to find the number we need for all the dates that we need them."

Jerry wasn't just his friend, he was in the company the same as Adam. Only, Adam had bought the company and started wearing suits to meetings with clients. Jerry was clear he didn't want the headache or the ties. But he was the best advice Adam could find. He sighed out a breath. "Okay. Let's do one more search and see if we can find sub-rentals. Also, put Tommy on it. I don't know why, but everybody likes that kid. They'll bend over backward to get him whatever equipment he needs. He's like some lost puppy."

He shouldn't have said that, but Jerry grinned. "Good point. I'm on it."

"Let me know tomorrow by noon, and we'll make a final decision."

With that, Jerry was out the door and Adam was sitting in his office, head in his hands, just like he'd started, but now with more to worry about. His brain had not been in the game for almost two weeks, not since the Nashville Brewers Fest.

Hailey.

He'd told himself long ago that he was over her. He'd believed that if he saw her again, she'd just be a girl he used to know. But it hadn't gone down that way—Jesus, it had *not* gone down that way.

Looking through the contracts spread across his desk for upcoming jobs, he saw that none of them could get signed and finished tonight. It was Thursday. If he waited until Friday, Knoxville would clog up and getting out to see his mother would be even harder.

Fuck it, he thought and stood up to leave. One thing Clayton had taught him was not to let the job run his life. It was a lesson that he hadn't listened to often enough.

This job paid his mother's medical bills. It covered his father's funeral last year. Just six months ago Adam had gotten himself out from under most of six years of debt. He'd paid off his own car—bought used from a dealer so it was in good shape. He got his mother into something a little bit better to drive and he was still paying on that. He gave his mother money for everything—bills, repairs, sometimes even groceries. She worked, but it didn't pay well, and his father hadn't left much behind. His parents had never had quite enough money to send his sisters to college. Adam had pitched in.

His salary at Clayton Light and Images had made it possible even before he'd bought the place. Tiffany had graduated a local state school with a bachelor's degree and was now working. She was married and on her own—for that Adam was grateful. It was a checkmark on a years-long list.

Rachel had just gotten her associates degree, and she was heading off to nursing school next. Another checkmark. The family had agreed to help her with her undergraduate work, but for nursing school, she would need to take out loans. She was excited, and he'd been excited to write that last check to cover her tuition. Even Chelsea was doing well. All of his sisters were now more educated than he was, at least formally.

It had been worth it, he'd made a difference. His sisters had been able to go to school. His parents hadn't lost their house or had to declare bankruptcy. He was confident that his mother's ongoing illness contributed to his father's heart attack the year before, but he was also confident that it would have come much sooner without the financial relief his staying behind and working had afforded them.

Adam reminded himself of this as he drove out of town, as the stoplights slowly and slowly got further apart. The road separated itself from the basic grid of the city and began twisting. The pavement now followed the hills and hollows where he'd grown up.

He passed churches with ground level signs that somebody put the letters into each week. He drove down long, winding streets where the houses changed style on each lot. Vast, plantation style homes sat next to old, four-room squares whose roofs sagged in the middle. Every tenth house had a junkyard in the front. One had old rusted tractors, another held classic cars damaged enough as to make anyone who loved a good antique cry as they drove by.

If Adam turned left, he would head down to the trailer park, where Hailey had grown up. Instead, he turned right, taking the road to the house where he'd grown up. His mother greeted him at the door.

"Hey, baby!" Her hands came up and clasped his face. She looked older. These last few years had been hard on her. He smiled but his mind flashed through to Hailey.

He'd lost Hailey for his mom and he thought at the time that it was a good trade. He hadn't asked Hailey not to go—only to wait a few years so he could take care of his mother. Hailey hadn't been willing to stay. Not even for a while.

She was so confident in his mother's willingness to manipulate all her children that she hadn't believed his mother actually had cancer.

"Come on in," his mother said with an overly wide grin. "I made meatloaf casserole. Your favorite."

It wasn't his favorite. He did like it, but over the years, it had lost that status. It had come to mean that she had a favor she wanted to ask. "What do you need done, Mom? Let me help."

Fifteen minutes later, while the smell of baking casserole wafted up to him, Adam stood in the attic, covered in dust and regretting that he'd asked. This was why she'd made the casserole.

Meatloaf casserole was a lot of work—he knew. First, she had to make meatloaf. Then there was the assembly and baking of the dish. Yeah, she could have done the job here in the attic. In fact, she was smaller. She fit the space better than his tall frame did. But she'd rather make a casserole and ask him to do it. She'd played the "bad back" card, and then added, "Just leave it if you don't want to do it. Maybe your sister can do it when she gets here."

He now coughed hard three times as he mistakenly breathed in too hard. The attic had clearly been visited frequently but not dusted. *Jesus.*

Hailey had been wrong—his mother had cancer—but she hadn't been wrong about his mother.

13

Hailey sat on her couch, her guitar resting on her knees. As she leaned forward, she pulled the coffee table up closer and laid out several pencils. Then scribbled whatever she came up with.

She knew the rule. If she counted any number of songs on the radio, the vast majority of them would be about love—finding it, losing it, being dumb and throwing it away. So she figured she could milk this emotional upsurge she was dealing with for at least three songs.

Brenda agreed. In fact, Hailey had told Brenda far too much about her relationship with Adam, and not even in the kind of way that one would tell a friend confiding a secret and feeling better at the end. No, Brenda had just wanted to know which pieces of it they could milk for the best songs. So here Hailey was, bleeding again—actively throwing herself back into her high school days. Back to the small trailer and the inability to completely close her door or have someone not watching over her shoulder. To nights of sneaking out and putting a sleeping bag in the bed of Adam's father's truck and thinking no one knew what they were doing.

It was eleven a.m. on a Tuesday, and she would have been down at the Heart Beats studio, except for the issue that all the rooms were booked right now. She had an appointment for later in the afternoon, but when the urge struck, it struck. By the time she started writing the thoughts and sounds down, Hailey was glad she was at home.

It was hard bleeding for her work. Maybe she didn't need anyone peering through a window to see how she was doing or waving and smiling and striking up a conversation. Picking up her coffee to take a sip, she instantly felt that the cup was far too light to have anything left in it. Setting her guitar aside, she stood up. Maybe she didn't need coffee, maybe what she needed was a beer. She was at home and she wasn't going anywhere.

Honestly, if she was going to bleed for her work, she deserved something harder than a coffee. The writing might even go a little better if she was a little looser. Grabbing a beer from the back of the fridge, Hailey popped the top and took a long pull.

Ah, yes, this was what she needed.

She headed back to the couch, plunking the beer onto a coaster and setting the guitar back across her knees. She was in cutoff jean shorts and a tank top, her red hair thrown back over her shoulder. The air conditioning was turned to a temperature higher than she would have liked in hopes of not having a bill that was higher than she was willing to pay. The beer definitely helped with the heat and the heat helped with throwing her back to her high school days and the time she'd spent tumbling head over heels for Adam.

She drifted back to her first kiss. That had been third grade, Timmy Higgins, and it had been a mess. Definitely not song worthy. She thought about combining several experiences into one song. No one would know. But, as she thought back over a series of first kisses, nothing played out with any drama until she got to Adam.

She thought about the high school hallway and the first time she'd seen him. It had been the third time she'd seen the hot boy in the grade ahead of her that he had finally looked up and seen her, too. Later, he told her he'd noticed her red hair and the curls. She'd put far too much time and hairspray into her hair the next morning. To this day, it was a decision that she never regretted. Still, it had taken another month for him to kiss her.

She'd been waiting.

She'd kissed other boys before, so Hailey had not been shy. When Adam had leaned in gingerly for that first kiss, Hailey had thought she'd known what to expect.

She'd been wrong.

Setting her guitar aside and leaning back on the couch, she tried to let the memory wash over her while still keeping it at arm's distance.

That didn't work.

Brenda was right. It wasn't enough to watch it play out in her mind, she had to re-*live* it. That's what made the song amazing.

She sank further into the memory. They'd been under a stairwell at the high school. Probably more drugs had been traded there than kisses. They'd gone on three dates, all of which had ended awkwardly. Hailey had had enough waiting—he either wanted to kiss her or he didn't—and she was going to find out.

She was the one who had led him around the corner. "Adam, are you ever going to kiss me?" He hadn't answered, not with words. Simply pulled her books from her hands, set them on the floor, and tugged her into his arms. It was the hardest, sweetest kiss she'd ever gotten. He turned her insides to jelly and melted her heart.

Then and now.

He'd been awkward before, but maybe he'd only needed to know that she *wanted* to kiss him. That kiss had left her dazed to the point where he'd had to lean over, pick up her schoolbooks and put them back in her hands. He'd told her she was about to be late to class. As her eyes glazed from the memory, her body felt the touch of him all over again. The memories were still so strong.

When she pulled them out, they swamped her. Which was maybe why she'd avoided doing exactly this over the last handful of years. Now, she leaned forward, scratched a handful of words onto the page, plucked a few chords, and tried it again and again until the song matched the feelings.

The problem was, three verses later, she wasn't remembering things that had happened—she was *fantasizing*. She lived an alternate life that might have happened had she stayed.

Adam insisted they would just wait a few years, that they would leave as soon as his mother was better. But even at that young age, Hailey had known better. If his mother wasn't going to let him go then, she wouldn't let him go in three years either. Hailey would have wound up singing at weddings and funerals, maybe opening a few ballgames at the school. If she was lucky, she might get all the way to Knoxville.

That was the life she'd rejected. But the other part of the fantasy was what gave her pause: a house, a picket fence, a yard. Two little girls, red hair like hers. Dark chocolate eyes like Adam's.

Just like that, she was lost, thinking about what might have been.

He had chosen his mother over her. She had chosen her career over him. But had she also chosen it over an entire life that she would never get to live now? Maybe she had.

Hailey was sucking in a deep breath—whether it was one of regret or confidence that she'd made the right decision, she didn't know—and she was startled from her reverie as a knock came at the door. She wasn't expecting anyone, and her first thought was that the food delivery had gotten an apartment address wrong again.

She was pulling open the door, ready to say, "You want three-oh-four not four-oh-four" when she stopped dead.

Adam stood in her doorway.

The blue suit showed off the depth in his eyes. The shock of dark hair showed he'd been running his fingers through it as though he'd been stressed. The loosened tie around his neck told her he decided to go into work this morning but had somehow wound up here.

Had he come all this way from Knoxville?

He opened his mouth to say hello and whatever else might have followed, she wouldn't ever know. Reaching out on an impulse borne of all the things she'd been imagining, Hailey grabbed the front of his shirt and dragged him into the apartment.

14

A dam stepped willingly into the apartment as Hailey's hand grabbed his shirt and tugged him through the doorway. Backing up as she pulled him forward, she used her free hand to push the door closed behind him.

Before he could open his mouth to say why he was here, her mouth was on his and he melted into the feeling.

Her hands, once tugging him inside, now pushed his shoulders. For a moment he resisted until he realized she was working to get his suit jacket off. With a shrug, he let it fall to the floor behind him. Her deft fingers found the buttons on the front of his shirt, and she leaned into him again as their tongues tangled.

Before he realized what he was doing, he'd slid his fingers under the hem of the tank top she wore. The heat of skin just above the waist of her almost-too-short jeans made him suck in a breath. He could almost feel the humidity of the tent from the Brewers Fest again. He could feel the cosmic pull of being inside her and was suddenly tugging her shirt up and over her head, revealing another lacy bra.

She pulled back barely an inch, her breasts heaving against

him. The words tumbled out of his mouth before he could stop them. "Do you always wear these?"

His fingers were touching her without thought, without hesitation, and without permission. But she leaned into his hand and her eyes fell half closed as she whispered back, "Only when I'm thinking about you."

His brain caught at the thought and he could feel blood rushing toward his already hard cock. What she did to him. She could turn him on with a look, a word, even just a breath.

With a deep heave of his lungs for air, he dove at her again, the two of them pushing toward each other, fingers searching, as Hailey walked them backward toward an open door.

Bedroom, he thought. *Let it be a bedroom.*

He caught only the smallest glimpses of the place as she tugged him along. The living room, the dining area, and the open kitchen were all cluttered. A guitar laid on the couch where she must have set it to get the door. Others waited patiently in their stands beneath the window. She had papers strewn across the coffee table. One empty beer bottle sat on the counter and another—seemingly more freshly opened—was waiting patiently on the coffee table.

All of that disappeared as she tucked a finger into the front of his pants, the only thing left to grab him by. All the rest of his clothing had been abandoned, but Hailey didn't let that stop her as she pulled him into a quiet oasis. The bedroom was done in shades of pale grey and silver. A white comforter added to the feeling of tranquility and the two of them tumbled downward onto it together, mouths fused, bodies and limbs entwined.

Her hands came up, cupping either side of his head and making him look her in the eyes. He hadn't even managed to reply to her questioning "Hello?" as she'd opened the door, so she was now giving him a chance to…

What?

Back out? *Hell no.* He was half naked and she wasn't naked

enough. He dove back at her, his mouth searching the breasts that had always fascinated him. Were they larger than when she'd been in high school? He was still a sucker for every part of her.

Reaching around her back as she arched up, he flicked open the three hooks at the back of the bra and peeled it down her arms before flinging it across the room. It seemed fitting to use his skills on the woman who'd taught him so much.

She moaned his name, only the second word spoken between them, and arched her back again. He knew what she wanted, but he knew what he wanted, too.

Their interlude in the tent had been amazing—mind-blowing and unexpected. But this? Now? He wanted to slow down.

"Hold on, baby. In a bit." He whispered the words as it hit him that he *knew* her. This wasn't some woman he was having sex with, this was *the woman* who'd taught him how to give and take pleasure. They'd experimented on each other with reckless abandon as teenagers, and he now knew that she would beg him. *More. Harder. Faster.*

Adam also knew he could hold back and make her scream.

Ignoring the deep certainly in his chest that this wasn't just about the sex, he pushed her back onto the comforter and began his way downward. Flicking the button on her cut-off jeans he tugged while she wiggled out of them and so easily back into his heart.

Had he ever stopped loving her?

"Adam! *Please.*" She whimpered the word and he ignored what it did to him.

It wasn't the time to ask himself any deep questions.

"Soon."

15

Adam was still breathing heavily as he finally glanced up to the ceiling. He wanted to believe that he didn't know what she'd done to him. But he did know. She was Hailey, and they were like this. Like nothing else he'd ever known.

Thinking clearly—or *more clearly* than he'd been thinking, since before he decided to hang a righthand turn and head to Hailey's apartment unannounced—Adam took a deep breath. Driving the extra few blocks, he'd planned it all out: knock on the door and hope she was home. He'd even pulled a sticky note from the glove box and shoved it in his pocket to leave on the door in case she wasn't.

In his original plan, he would ask her out on a date. He might even fold and say it was just old friends getting together. Whatever it was, it needed to make up for him suggesting she might run off pregnant with his child and hide it from him. Since he'd had time to think, he'd cringed several times over that massive blunder and he wasn't going to make it again.

Adam thought he would speak when he got his breathing under control, but he couldn't quite seem to do it. It took another few minutes before he could tell her, "This wasn't what I intended to happen."

Beside him, tucked up close, his arm around her, her head on his shoulder, Hailey was easy to read. He felt her answer as she merely shrugged in response. Silence accompanied his wait as he tried to think of something else to say.

But it was Hailey, and it only took another moment of almost-awkward space before she popped onto one elbow and look down at him, her brows pulling together. "How did you know where I live?"

"I looked you up. You're not hard to find."

"Were you in Nashville today for something else?"

He nodded to that one. Seeing that Hailey was on a roll, and he was going to get barraged by questions until she had all the answers she wanted, he turned his head until he was looking directly at her. But she was already locked and loaded with the next one.

"Did you have a job out here?"

"Yes. With Hilton."

He hadn't quite gotten the whole Hilton job sorted out yet. So he'd needed to come out and speak to the manager face to face. When he'd hit the edge of town it had simply been too tempting to make the turn and head this way. Instead, Adam forced himself to go to the meeting first. After that he was *supposed* to drive home.

But—though he could go back and forth in one day—it wasn't a short trip from Knoxville to Nashville. So he'd very easily talked himself into showing up here.

"Are you working tonight?" Her next question came out in rapid-fire words.

Adam shook his head, his breathing rough and heart rate speeding up again. Would she do his work for him and ask *him* to dinner?

But she didn't, not right away. Instead, she lowered herself back down into the crook of his arm, snuggling close in a gesture that felt all too familiar, and was far too easy to settle into, despite the years apart.

Surely, she had dated in the interim. Maybe she'd even done something as crazy as gotten married and then divorced. He had dated and had one serious, ongoing relationship. It wasn't until his mother started to pressure him to marry Janet that he truly understood that Janet was absolutely not the right woman for him.

His mother had not been fond of Hailey. Her subsequent love of Janet had been all he'd needed to realize that he and Janet didn't have a relationship worth keeping.

That had been two years ago. In the meantime, there had been about twenty, maybe thirty, first dates. There had been very few second dates. It must have been his thoughts rolling roughshod over his own past that made the words tumble out of his mouth. "Are you seeing anyone?"

His head turned involuntarily, because he wanted to see her face before she answered. It would probably be the truest answer he would get.

What he got was one raised eyebrow. "Adam Zucker, I would not be naked in bed with you if I was seeing someone else."

He had to wonder why he insisted on keeping talking. It was only going to hurt him if she said anything, but he asked anyway. "You could be seeing someone and maybe it's not serious. Maybe you just broke up and you're rebounding. Maybe there's someone you're pursuing, but it hasn't happened yet." He paused, mentally poising the knife at his own heart in case she wanted to push it in. "Any of those?"

Hailey barked out a laugh. "Adam, I don't have time to pursue *anyone*. And therefore I didn't have time to date anyone and recently break up."

Her answer settled in his chest like a heavy rock. It should have made him feel better that she didn't belong to someone.

That he wasn't just a rebound fuck. The deep-seated jealousy shouldn't have taken hold, but it did.

This was pure Hailey—too busy for a relationship. She'd even been too busy for the one she'd had with him years ago. Lord knew, she'd walked out the door as fast as she could. The smart thing for him to do would be to climb out of bed, kiss her softly, tell her thank you, and *just leave*. He'd already tangled himself up far too much with a woman who'd proven she wouldn't wait for him. Not even for a little while. He should have told her he was leaving.

He didn't do any of those things. The words that came out of his mouth were, "Would it be okay if I took you out to dinner?"

16

Hailey bit into the piece of fried chicken and let the heat suffuse through her mouth. It almost hurt—the perfect level of spice tempered under a layer of syrup. She should not be eating this, but Adam had wanted to do something purely *Nashville*. Of course, that meant she took him out for hot chicken and waffles.

"You're a spice pansy," she told Adam who sat beside her, crunching into his own much, much milder piece of chicken. Making fun of him was a prerequisite given their past.

They'd slid back into a relationship—whatever it was—as easily as they'd slid into the booth. The touch of his arm against hers, the rub of his suit pants against her nice jeans, all triggered the sweetly rolling feelings inside her. Feelings that she shouldn't be having. She'd been trying to combat all her feelings by asking questions. Safe questions.

"How's your friend Jerry?" "How are your sisters doing?" "Did Rachel ever get to nursing school like she wanted?"

But Adam was having none of that. Instead, he cut into his waffle swirling the piece into the syrup. Before taking a bite, he turned and asked, "Are we a thing again?"

She'd just taken a bite of her own chicken. The heat filling her sinuses now hit the pain level and she shrugged. "I don't know what we are Adam."

Why was he ruining good food with conversation like this?

"I don't know if I could define it if I tried." She ate the next bite of waffle as nonchalantly as a woman could when she'd just been asked to define an undefinable relationship.

But Adam still wasn't satisfied. He paused mid-bite and stared at her as though he knew she had more to say. She had no idea what any of it meant, or what it would mean for their future—a future she was certain they didn't have.

He owned a business now. More than ever, he was *stuck* here in Tennessee. She had a tour coming up. Despite her truncated dates, she was still going to be gone more than she was home. She had an album to rehash and release. With any luck, there would be radio interviews and more.

"It's easy," she told him, wondering if he would interpret that "easy" was all they were. "We already know each other. We know what each other likes—"

He interrupted her, his words a deep rumble of syrup and whiskey that pulled at her insides a little more. "Yeah, we do."

"Do we keep seeing each other like this?" she asked. This sucked. What if he said *no*? But she ignored the knot in her chest and waited.

He finally took the bite, chewed, then shrugged.

"You mean, where I come into your room or your dressing room and we act like maniacs?" He smiled as he said it, something she hadn't quite expected. He wanted a physical relationship and probably not much more.

The bite of chicken went down like a knot, but she tried to keep a neutral expression as his head tilted a little to the side. She must be taking longer to answer than he planned. Quickly, she shoved another bite of chicken into her mouth, this time enjoying the pain of the heat as it radiated outward.

She shouldn't be disappointed. After all, what had she really expected? They'd screwed in her dressing room tent. It was entirely possible people had been walking by on the other side of the thin plastic walls. It was possible they'd heard everything. When he had showed up at her apartment, she'd pulled him into the bedroom and practically ripped his clothing off before he could say a word.

The first time she could blame on him, but the second? That was all on her. So, of course, he wanted a physical relationship and she found herself nodding along.

Having sex with Adam sure didn't hurt. And when had she ever met anyone who could touch her the way that he did?

He grinned a sly smile she immediately recognized—one that said he'd gotten what he wanted. "Do we need to set some ground rules?"

The question almost made her choke.

Jesus. She had once loved this man so much that she thought she would spend the rest of her life with him. Even in high school, he cheered her on and wanted the best for her. When he could have been jealous of her successes, he never was. When it took work on both of their parts, he happily did more than his share. He'd had his own dreams, too. Adam played a little guitar and used to joke about being her backup. But mostly, he'd been interested in producing music—more pop than country. But still, Nashville and L.A. would have been equally good to him.

Instead, he'd been too devoted to a family that Hailey had always seen as taking far more than it gave. In spite of all of that, and all the time apart, she had to admit now that she'd always believed if they ever came back around, they would be the real deal. They would have everything. Instead, here she was introducing him to chicken and waffles and setting up ground rules for how they screwed.

But Adam was already talking, and she figured she'd better listen.

"—no one else. Just us. If you want to be with someone else, we have to break up. I don't share well. I'll afford you the same." He tacked on the last part, reminding her that it wasn't going to be all about what she wanted and when she wanted him. "I'm clean. I've been tested. You?"

She nodded around another bite of chicken that should have tasted far better than this conversation. "Yes. And I'm on birth control. What else do you want?"

She watched his eyes widen at her sharp tone and she quickly wished she'd reined in her irritation. It was time to flatten her expression—*past time*—and act like a big girl.

Getting back together with Adam, even just physically, was easy. She knew who he was, and what to expect. Now, he was simply laying out the rules to make things clear. He wasn't at fault.

Besides, Adam did know how to put a smile on her face. So, she faked a grin and said, "We don't need condoms." Then she agreed to not sleep with anyone else. She said it as though it was a concession of some sort rather than something that would happen whether or not she was sleeping with Adam. "How often are you likely to be in town?"

This arrangement was a good thing. So why did her heart kick so hard?

17

H ailey spent that night alone.

Eventually they'd managed to get off the sticky topic of how much sex they could be having, and the conversation had at last become easy. The knot in Hailey's chest had loosened, and she talked without censoring her words or faltering.

Though it did seem they had some implicit agreement that they would not talk about what they had just done. Setting the ground rules had apparently been enough and they'd moved on to safer topics. But as the meal wore on, Hailey began waffling about whether to ask him to stay overnight with her.

Ultimately, she was sure that she wanted him to stay, but she wasn't sure if she wanted to deal with the consequences. He must have seen her discomfort because he paid the check at the end of the meal and said, "I need to hit the road and get back to Knoxville tonight."

He'd dropped her at her apartment door with just a quick kiss. Turning, he headed back to his car and back to his other life, seemingly without any regrets.

She'd rolled around in bed that night unsure how she felt about all the big things they'd decided. She'd mused about the fact that these weren't supposed to be big changes yet, somehow, they were.

She didn't hear from Adam the next day. Or the next, or the next.

Originally, she'd been scheduled to leave on the first leg of the tour, but instead she was home. Adam knew this. She'd told him —*hadn't she?* Well, she wasn't about to message him her schedule when he'd made it clear they weren't like that. So Brenda sent Wilder out on the road for a week and left Hailey behind with her guitar, still asking her to bleed for two more songs.

Hailey was getting close on the second song—the one about the path not taken. She was considering just calling it "Unexpected." The song certainly was taking her by surprise. She'd thought she would sing about what had happened between them. Instead, the music came out gloriously upbeat, only to get to the last verse and realize the family was all the concoction of a woman who had given it away in favor of her own career.

Hailey was working hard not to make it a regretful tune. She didn't regret any of her decisions to get where she was, and she knew tons of women who didn't either. It was just about wondering what the other road might have held. In her song, the only regrets were for chances not taken.

"Oh shit! Yes!" She'd jumped up off the couch the moment she'd thought of it. She'd knocked her beer over and hadn't cared because the carpet in her apartment was cheap anyway. "Yes!"

What if could be huge. And she wasn't going to let anyone know it was a what-if song until the last verse. Yes! *Yes, yes, yes!*

She and Brenda worked hard on finding the fine line on beat and tempo in tone. And Hailey was still walking the fine line of writing other wistful, wishful songs about Adam while waiting for him to show back up in her bed. But he didn't, and she was on the road before she knew it.

When she got her first text from him five days later, she almost laughed out loud.

—I'm in Nashville tomorrow. You around?

—Nope, she replied quickly. —You just missed me. I'm on the tour bus.

Two hours out of town, she thought. *His loss.*

His next text came back quickly, as though once he had decided to talk to her he was simply waiting for her replies.

—Where to?

—Pennsylvania, New York, New Jersey.

She could almost hear him laughing in the return beep that signaled his message had arrived. —They do country music up there?

—They do country music everywhere, Honey.

"Who are you talking to?"

Hailey's head snapped up as though she'd been caught at something, and she hoped it didn't show on her cheeks. Her drummer, Carrie, had one arm propped on the back of the seat in front of her and was looking down at Hailey.

"What?" She'd been so focused on the phone conversation, that she almost hadn't even processed that someone was speaking to her.

"I don't know," Carrie drew the words out with a sly smile. "But you were looking at your phone and grinning wildly."

Luckily that was all Carrie had to say about that. With a knowing tilt of her head, she walked further back down the bus and left Hailey sitting there. She had spread out on the couch behind the fold out table, in full view of anyone up and moving around.

She'd thought traveling with an all-female band was going to be amazing. On the one hand, it was. On the other hand, she was realizing she would be able to keep zero secrets. Carrie, at least, was going to have it all figured out if Hailey didn't work hard at keeping her thoughts in check.

Her phone chimed again.

—Country Music was born in Pennsylvania?

—Oh please. She tapped it out with her thumbs. Every place that's not a big city thinks they invented country music. And they think they own it. All their news stations call their local area the "Heartland."

She was rewarded for her quote marks with a large laughing-until-it-cried face.

—Well then. Have fun in the heartland.

She was grinning as the phone immediately chimed again and one more line came through.

—Knock'em dead, Baby.

She wanted to smile. She wanted to send back a heart, and she wanted to steel herself against everything a stupid text had made her feel. Because she wasn't supposed to be feeling anything.

18

Well, crap, Adam thought, setting his phone down on his desk.

He thought he'd been playing it cool. He hadn't reached out and neither had she. It seemed they were both okay with this "just physical" arrangement they'd set up.

In the final tally, Adam was starting to wonder if he wasn't.

Though he hadn't reached out to her, he'd had to constantly remind himself that he didn't have any reason to be in Nashville. And that he shouldn't invent one. He'd thought about her every single day. If he was being honest, he spent more moments thinking about Hailey than he had thinking about the business he'd worked so hard to build.

If he was being *very* honest, this wasn't anything new.

He'd always thought about her. He thought about her when she was with him, and he thought about her for the eight years they hadn't spoken.

He'd lived so much of his life around her, he'd believed she was just an embedded part of his history. But now that he'd seen her again, it was getting harder to make that excuse.

He had a year and a half of Community College under his

belt, because of Hailey. He'd wanted to wait until she graduated before transferring to whatever college they picked together. He could have gone off on his own when he'd graduated, and his life would certainly have been different if he had.

It would have been much harder to come back home and take a factory job, if his mother's diagnosis had come in while he'd been way. But he hadn't been far away—he'd had to be within arm's reach of Hailey. He'd stayed close to Carroll Hollow for her. But even after she was long gone, he'd still thought about her.

Now that she was back in his life, he found himself making decisions based on Hailey once more.

He'd sent Jerry on the last trip to Nashville, just so he wouldn't doubt his own motives. He'd actively refrained from texting her, just so he wouldn't look too eager. And now, when he was going to be in Nashville, she was gone for several weeks. Adam wasn't going to see her, and it was his own damn fault.

He turned his gaze back to the Hilton job. The contract had been signed. Sub rentals for the equipment had been found, though Jerry was still trying to talk him into buying several million dollars worth of heavy equipment.

Adam had been crunching the numbers for days. Like his arrangement with Hailey, it looked good on paper. Like his arrangement with Hailey, he told himself he could live with the consequences.

Unlike his arrangement with Hailey, he was beginning to feel that he should throw himself in headfirst. Only with Hailey, he wasn't supposed to want that as much as he did.

19

"**P**it stop!" the bus driver called out, making Hailey's head pop up.

They now were three shows into an eleven-show section of the tour. Then she would go home, and Wilder would pick up the next dates while she continued to rework her album according to Brenda's specifications.

"Where are we?" she asked.

"Middle of nowhere," the driver called back. But Hailey saw a sign for a small town and a few white farmhouses in the distance. They had passed a handful of barns with Pennsylvania Dutch signs over the doorways. "Looks like it's called True Springs."

Rhea, their driver, kept a lax hand on the large steering wheel. Whatever was happening to make them take an unscheduled stop, it didn't bother her.

Right then Hailey's phone rang. "Melissa?" she said by way of greeting, putting the phone to her ear.

Melissa was managing this leg of the tour. The call wasn't unusual, until Melissa began explaining the new problem with the second of the two buses. "Look, Hailey, my trailer is having issues. There's a small repair shop in the next town... I called ahead and the good news is that the management thinks they can handle it today."

Melissa sighed, and Hailey wondered why she was even included in this decision. She was the "talent," but the talent's opinion mattered a hell of a lot less than people thought.

"We have a couple of options," Melissa continued, making the issue clear relatively quickly. "We can stay on schedule. Mostly. Either way, we'll have to take a short stop here in True Springs. But if you want to keep moving, we're going to have to double up the people on the bus. The equipment bus is fine, so at least that's not an issue."

That was when Hailey understood. There were three buses on this tour. The first, hers, carried the band. The second held Melissa and her two roadies. The third was almost people-free, carrying the equipment packed in tight.

So Melissa was explaining to her the logistics. If they kept driving, Hailey would have to deal with the fact that her bus would be severely overcrowded. There was no extra room in the equipment bus—certainly not for people. It would add to an already cramped situation, and probably increase the stress factor on the first leg of her first tour.

"Also," Melissa continued, "They'll need their luggage and it won't entirely fit underneath. In fact, only a little of it will."

Hailey wanted to cringe. That was in large part her own fault. She was the lead, which that meant she was traveling with her own clothes and several costume changes. She'd had Shay make her several versions of each one in case of damage or dirt or God knew what. But it was a lot to haul around.

"If we do that, we can stay to our driving schedule." Melissa pushed on, not seeing Hailey's cringe.

"Sleeping will be really awkward," Hailey pointed out.

"Absolutely," was Melissa's only reply.

There were a limited number of beds on the bus. They'd all have to share and sleep in shifts.

"Option number two?" Hailey asked.

"Stay in True Springs and get eight hours behind schedule or however long it takes them to fix this bus. And hope that they can get it fixed in time to get us back on the road and late for rehearsal but not the show."

"What do you think we should do?" Hailey asked.

"I think it's about how crowded you are willing to be and how much being late affects you." She paused, then added, "I think it's anybody's guess how quickly they're going to be able to fix this monster." Melissa referred to the second bus, the one that she was on, and the one that was apparently making concerning noises and overheating.

In the end, they opted for a halfway check. They would stay in True Springs for four hours, and then check again on the repairs on the bus and see what they needed to do. Hailey liked that she had options. "Then we can make a decision based on whether or not they still think they can get the other bus running in time."

It was only twenty minutes before the chain of tour buses pulled off the exit and disgorged all the people in front of an adorable little inn. Hailey stepped into summer air that was hot, but milder than the oppressive humidity she was used to. She was looking around when she felt her drummer grab her hand and pull her along.

Grinning, Carrie told them, "Grab your pennies, ladies, there's a fountain!"

Hailey laughed as the buses pulled away to find the local mechanic and the women stopped in front of a trickling fountain. "I didn't figure you for the wishing fountain kind, Carrie."

Carrie was wearing black leather pants and a tank top that laced up the sides. She definitely stood out in True Springs, but she was already digging for pennies from her wallet. "Oh, I'm not. But we need to do everything we can to get that bus repaired!"

20

Hailey's phone pinged with a message from Adam.

— Where are you today?

She could feel one side of her lips quirk up as Carrie looked at her.

Her drummer raised a pierced eyebrow from over her magazine. "I wish I got a message like that."

"Sadly, it's not like that. I wish." Hailey turned her phone around to show Carrie. "He wanted to know where we are today. And look where we are." She waved her hands around the small gift shop.

After the women had tossed every penny—and a handful of nickels and dimes—into the True Springs fountain, Carrie had poked around and called out, "Look at this. It's a plaque."

She'd proceeded to read it out loud to Hailey and Melissa about how the water was believed to bring anyone who drank it their true love. "That's *True Love* with capital letters."

Hailey had snorted, but Carrie immediately reached into the water and splashed Melissa. "If you get it in your mouth, you'll find your true love!" She scooped more water and flicked it at their manager again.

"Uh!" Melissa looked affronted for a moment, but as Hailey watched, determination set into her gaze and she returned fire on Carrie. There was something in her expression that made Hailey wonder if it was true, that no one could resist a drummer. Was the water already working on these two? She stepped back out of reach of the splashes. The last thing Hailey needed was a complication like *True Love*.

After a moment, her manager and drummer called a truce, deciding to quit before they actually got wet, rather than just spotted with fountain water. They'd looked around for the next adventure to bide their time in True Springs and found a shop, where they'd wandered aimlessly, looking at trinkets until Hailey's text had caught Carrie's eye.

"Is that your *True Love*?" Carrie pressed, the tone in her voice clearly capitalizing the *true* and *love* parts.

It was all Hailey could do to avoid saying, "I think it's my Fuck Buddy." Because the fact was, at one point, Adam had been her *True Love*. Capital T. Capital L. The corner of her mouth dropped instantly.

"It should be!" The voice coming from behind her startled her and took her a moment to figure out that when Hailey hadn't answered Carrie, the voice did. "You'll find your true love if you drink from that fountain. It's the best kept secret in the state."

"Oh," Hailey turned around, the question she wanted to ask hovering on her lips as her eyes scanned empty air. At last they came to rest on the very short woman in front of her. Silver hair and knuckles that spoke of arthritis didn't detract from sharp eyes and a wide smile.

Hailey heard Brenda's voice in her head. She was a public figure now, which meant that when she was in public she had to be polite, charming, *on*. Even if people didn't know who she was, they might one day remember. She turned up the megawatt smile. "Well, we're very lucky we wound up in the best kept secret then. Because one of our tour buses has left us stranded for a bit."

"Yes! You are in luck." The woman's smile grew wider, if that was possible. "I'm Mabel and Mac runs the repair shop. He'll take good care of your truck or whatever. That boy can fix anything."

"Well, that's good to hear." Hailey was still smiling though she was looking for something else to say when Mabel turned away.

"Let me get you ladies some hot cocoa or coffee, if you prefer."

Hailey felt the corner of her mouth quirk again. It had been ages since anyone thought she was of an age to be offered a hot cocoa. The three women followed Mabel around toward the back of the small shop where a counter flanked a small area to prep coffee and sodas and maybe a scoop of ice cream.

Hailey watched as Mabel slowly and carefully mixed cocoa into one of the cups and poured coffee into two of the others, as Carrie and Melissa had requested. Hailey stared down in at the marshmallows swirling at the rich surface. It was not a cool day, but they were inside in the air conditioning, surrounded by the tchotchkes and the sweet old lady. She could drink hot cocoa and make an old lady happy.

For a moment, the three women just sat at the counter, taking sips and looking around before Mabel said into the air, apropos of nothing, "I made those drinks with fountain water for you."

It was Melissa who sputtered first. Hailey might have spit her cocoa back out...*if* she believed. But there was no way a fountain could hold the kind of magical properties that the plaque suggested. Surely it was there just to get people to throw in as much money as possible. The town would collect it and keep the fountain pretty, the flowers watered, and a little bit of a tourist trade going.

Hailey smiled a "thank you" at Mabel even though she didn't believe at all and raised her mug in a small salute before drinking again.

Beside her, Carrie elbowed Melissa. "Well, what do you

know?" she said, and made Hailey begin to wonder about the little encounter she'd seen back there at the edge of the fountain.

It wasn't any "magic" water working, it was just a spark of attraction being given a chance. Hell, the way things were going, hot cocoa made with a little bit of fountain water wasn't going to cut it for Hailey. She would need to fall in and practically drown to fix her love life.

Sure, she and Adam had heat, but aside from that, they'd been doomed from the start. It would have been better if he'd been some random guy working the show. Someone with whom she had instant chemistry and not much more.

Then again, none of it ever would have happened if he'd been random. She would never have done anything like that in her tent if it hadn't been someone she already trusted.

"You okay, honey?" Mabel asked.

"Oh, I'm good." She pulled out her phone and replied to Adam's text.

—I'm in a tiny town called True springs.

She didn't mention the water or its supposedly magical properties. She didn't tell him that she'd apparently been dosed by Mabel, who didn't seem to understand she'd already been splashed by Melissa and Carrie horsing around earlier. After a moment, when Adam didn't reply right away, Hailey figured he wouldn't. So she pushed the phone back into her pocket and finished the hot cocoa. Who knew how many hours they would be stuck here? Whether Mac the Wonder Mechanic could fix the tour bus.

So she wandered the store looking at all kinds of country paraphernalia. In the corner was a rack of quilts, one in beautiful shades of pinks and another in greens. A fall scene caught her eye on yet another quilt and she pulled it out to carefully admire both the work and the price tag. If she had money, she would take one. But not today.

The three women paid for their drinks and wandered until

they'd seen every last item the store offered. Later, when she plucked her phone out of her pocket again, Hailey saw that Adam had indeed replied and she missed it.

—I'm sorry I missed you before you left town. I was counting days and pretending I didn't want to call you and I screwed up. I should have just said I wanted to see you again.

Her heart stuttered a little.

Quickly. She sent a message back.

—Me too.

21

"Hey boss." Jerry stuck his head in the door where Adam had been sitting at his desk, staring at his phone. Before Adam could even answer, Jerry frowned and chimed in again. "You okay?"

This time, he took his own concern as cause to step into Adam's office and almost close the door behind him. He was clearly ready to offer a heart-to-heart that Adam probably needed but didn't want.

"Yeah, I'm good," Adam replied with a forced grin, though he knew he wasn't selling it. He could tell from Jerry's expression that Jerry wasn't buying either. But at least he offered only a nod and continued with what he'd come for.

"Did you ever make a decision on buying those projectors?"

Crap, Adam thought. This was exactly why Jerry wanted to know what was wrong with him. Something clearly was. He hadn't been himself lately, and it seemed everyone was picking up on it. The man Jerry knew was driven. He was going to build this business with everything he had. Adam showed up early and stayed late. Instead, what Jerry was getting now was the boss who had been staring at his computer and doing nothing for well over a week.

"I'll have the decision to you tomorrow," Adam told him and he meant it. It was well past time for him to get his head out of his ass. And his eyes off his cell phone.

"What you looking at?" Jerry asked.

And he couldn't even look away from the messages she wasn't sending him for a minute. Adam didn't want to answer, but maybe it would be better if he did. At least it would look better. He held his phone up face out toward his top guy.

"Oh, that's nice." Jerry grinned at a screen that showed him fifteen different women who had agreed to meet Adam via his online dating profile.

Adam smiled, but it probably didn't mean what Jerry thought it did. There were so many faces waiting for him because he hadn't checked in so long, not since before the Nashville Brewers Fest. He hadn't looked at his profile once since Hailey had crashed back into his life. What he was doing now was staring at it. Should he take his profile down?

He closed the app without making a decision. But it was making the messages pile up. Even his little decisions suddenly felt very big.

Jerry gave him a thumbs up sign and slipped out of the office, pulling the door mostly closed behind him. It was Adam's signal to his employees that he was busy but could be bothered for important things. The problem was that he wasn't actually busy, unless he counted staring at his phone and trying to answer basic questions about his own love life.

Apparently, he didn't have the answers to any questions at all. Should he or shouldn't he invest in the projectors? Should he or shouldn't he take down his online profile? Was he or wasn't he in a relationship with Hailey Watkins?

His phone pinged and he realized maybe he was. He had gone and confessed several hours ago that he missed her. He was definitely an idiot for playing games and counting days. And here she was saying she missed him too. So they *must* be involved.

Sure, he'd been staring at his phone like a lovesick fool for the last week, but he had also been taking a good hard look at his life. The return of Hailey Watkins was forcing him to ask some big questions. What was he doing with his life and what did he want?

Adam knew what he wanted to do with the company. He had the right job, at least. He probably wouldn't have been a good manager for Hailey's career, but he was a damn fine rigger and projectionist. He was an excellent cameraman and he'd become a good salesman. He prided himself on being a good boss. But for the rest of his life? He had no clue.

Was he a carefree bachelor dating wherever he felt like? Or was he looking for something real? It was hard to say. What did a guy do when he'd had something real at nineteen, but had been left with this?

For a moment, he thought about what he'd expected back then. He'd believed that by now Hailey would be a big star, that they'd definitely be married and probably be having children. They'd have a yard and a fence and maybe a minivan. None of that had come to pass.

Only Hailey was still on the right track. His path had changed entirely. Some of it was because of his mother, some of it was because he'd been nineteen and hadn't known what he was good at or what he wanted to do. Hell, he hadn't even known this career existed back then. Some of it was because he hadn't been able to see beyond Hailey Pulaski and her big dream of becoming a country star.

Everything had stayed the same for her, except him.

Everything had changed for him…except her.

But what did he want now? And did Hailey still fit into it? But even if she did fit into his dreams, did she want to?

22

Hailey rummaged through her purse at the counter of the small gas station. "I have change," she offered as she unzipped the compartment on her wallet only to find out she didn't.

Oh, yeah, she thought, *she'd thrown every last coin into the fountain at True Springs*. Right before the shopkeeper Mabel had made them drinks with fountain water.

Honestly, Carrie and Melissa looked like they'd already found whatever the fountain was promising. Hailey could admit she was more than a little bit jealous.

"Here." She gave up and handed over her card to buy the bag of chips and soft drink. Her diet had gone to hell.

Life on the road was harder than she'd thought it would be. She'd expected it to be grand rather than grinding. She loved being on stage, and she loved singing. But doing soundcheck wasn't singing—not like what she enjoyed. She wasn't the head-liner at any of these shows, so she was on and off stage often faster than she could blink. Sometimes she was on in the after-noon to crowds of people milling around and not paying atten-tion to the music. She sang her heart out anyway.

When it worked, the roar of the crowd lifted her up. Being able to sign a few posters and CDs afterwards—or even just knowing that she'd sold a good handful at the end of each show— made her smile. There were plenty of good times. Even being stuck in True Springs had turned out to be fun. But it was getting harder to get up on stage and give her all for a crowd that often didn't give anything in return.

Hailey was beginning to wonder if the stage and intermittent fun was enough to counteract the endless hours on the road, not being home, not being able to keep up with her friends or even get a cat or a dog... She must be losing it.

As she took her chips and climbed back up into the bus, it felt like every step was torture. Each high stair pulled her closer to the couch, the bunk bed with the thin curtain, the road rumbling under her so she could never quite just be *still*.

No, her emotions veered as wildly as the bus, swinging between sharp highs and deep boredom. When she was up, she breathed in the euphoria of being on stage, holding the mic out for the crowd to sing along to a chorus they had just learned, clapping over her head, and basically providing the energy for an entire festival and the occasional small arena. But when she was low, her thoughts were turning to the song she'd written. The "What if" one in which she sung about the other path she might have taken. Only now, she was thinking about it with regret.

Brenda had called four days ago and rerouted them. In the new venue tonight, Hailey had been the very first act, before the opening act of the opening act of the big band. The arena had been mostly dead when she and her band had gone out on stage, but the crew had graciously turned down the house lights, put the spotlight on her and let her sing her heart out. She'd done her best to fill the place with energy and music.

It had been beyond thrilling singing on an arena stage, even though she saw more empty chairs than faces. It was a definite checkmark on her list. She was on her way up, just as she'd planned.

But what she hadn't put on her checklist was the crippling depression of being cramped on the bus with the same four people for days on end. She smiled as Carrie and Melissa went by, their own bags of chips and cans of coke in their hands. Well, at least she wasn't the only one whose diet was going to hell.

Working out had been an unmitigated disaster, too. She'd tried the first handful of mornings to stand in the narrow aisle of the bus and do jumping jacks or at least some stretches. She hadn't tried again. Now, she was left to running the back hallways of the arena or a loop around the festival fairgrounds before she took a shower to go on stage. After doing her sound check she would take another shower. She'd do the same the next day, do the show. Shower. Hit the bus. This was what her life had been reduced to.

On top of all of it, she missed Adam terribly. Even when she'd first been on her own, right after she'd left him it had been easier not to miss him. Back then, she'd been so mad that the anger had fueled her, flinging her far out of Carroll Hollow and all the way into Nashville. It drove her to make her rent every month on time because she was going to show them all. She was driven, proving to an ex-boyfriend something he'd never see.

Now, she was on the road on her own bus. *Why didn't it feel better?*

Getting here had taken her years of steady improvement, even if it wasn't at the pace that she wanted or even what she'd expected. She reminded herself that the tour bus was something she dreamed of, even if her dream tour hadn't included the Cornbread Festival or being the opening- opening- opening-act.

She reached down into her purse to grab her phone to text Adam. She would have a conversation with him, not about how she missed him and not about how she really felt, but just to say

Hi. Just to ease the tight pressure in her chest. As she dug for the phone, her hand bumped the tiny, sealed Mason jar.

With a sigh, Hailey pulled it out and shook her head. This was the dumbest thing. Mabel had pulled her aside and pushed the adorable mini-jar into her hand.

"This is for you."

"What do I owe you?" Hailey asked though her mind had been elsewhere. Mabel was shrewd, telling them they needed drinks and then subtly letting them know there was a charge. Now she was pushing a product into Hailey's hand. Next on Hailey's checklist was learning how to graciously tell pushy old ladies "No thank you."

"You don't owe me anything." Mabel had curled Hailey's fingers around the jar. "You need this."

At the time Hailey hadn't looked at it. Carrie and Melissa were already out the door and about to leave her behind. She wondered if she'd been handed a jar of vodka or maybe even something illegal, but she'd shoved it into her purse, thanked Mabel for being a great hostess, and bolted after her friends.

Now, she could read the label on the jar in swooping, old fashioned cursive. If she hadn't dug Adam's grandmother's old letters out of his attic one day, she'd never have been able to read this. But it said, "True Springs Fountain Water." Under that, in smaller letters, Mabel had written "Take as needed."

Hailey pulled it out of her purse and pushed it down into the drawer built in under her bed. She didn't need to carry a jar around with her and it could stay here—out of the way—until she figured out what to do with Mabel's odd little "gift."

23

"Oh my God, are those for me?"

Adam's heart had thumped in his chest as Hailey smiled and reached out either for him or the flowers.

He couldn't tell which she wanted but showing up had worked in some way. He'd been standing here in the back parking lot at her label when she came off the tour bus, even though it was ten PM and she was supposed to have been in by eight.

Two hours, he'd been sitting out in the sultry Nashville night air, listening to cicadas. He wouldn't have thought they would be a problem in downtown Nashville, but the noise was loud when the streets were mostly empty.

It didn't matter that he waited two hours. He'd driven *three* to get here and he'd come into town early enough to stop and eat and get the flowers. He was clearly a fool, and he might as well admit it. But damn, she'd been gone for three weeks and he'd been the idiot who played his games and didn't call before she left. He did it to supposedly "cool off" after the hot and heavy night when they'd decided that they should at least be exclusive.

So he stood in the parking lot, leaning against his car and

playing with his phone as he waited. He'd set the flowers on the hood of the car but scooped them quickly into his hand each time a semi-large vehicle came down the back street.

This time, the bus pulled up and Hailey emerged, her eyes letting him know she was pleased to see him, but her actions said she was trying not to make a scene. Though he was clearly a lovesick fool, he tried not to act one hundred percent an idiot.

So he'd stepped back and watched silently as the others came down the steps, bags in hand. One woman, mostly in black, a piercing through her nose and a matching leather backpack slung over her shoulder, merely looked him up and down and said, "You must be Adam."

His heart swelled to think that at least someone knew who and what he was. He wondered what else Hailey might have said.

At some point, he'd decided she would hop off the bus and into his car and he would drive her home. But he'd never greeted a tour bus before, and he realized now that he should have played this smarter. His company ran trucks and he knew that when they showed up on site it often took several hours to unload. Sure enough, it took Hailey quite a while to get all her bags, check out with the manager, or do whatever the routine was while he stood around watching and waiting. He still had the flowers clutched in his grip until, at last, she turned to face him and he suddenly realized he'd been even more of a fool than he'd planned.

"It didn't even occur to me that you would have a ride." He blurted out the words even as he realized his mistake.

"My car is at my apartment. I was going to hit Cassie up." She motioned with her thumb over her shoulder. "But it appears Cassie has found another passenger."

With a quick glance beyond Hailey, Adam saw the two heads together, Cassie's red hair gleaming in the streetlight and another blonde head tucked up close to hers.

"Yeah, you would have been a third wheel there," he said, "but I can give you a ride." It was maybe the dumbest thing he'd ever said in his life, but Hailey's grin made it worth it.

At last, he pushed the flowers into her grip and climbed into the car. He had the engine on before he asked her, "Where do you want to go?"

Adam figured she'd say "home" and maybe fall asleep in the passenger seat, but instead she didn't say anything and he found himself offering up his own hotel. "I have a room at the Alton nearby."

The spark in her eyes had been worth every penny on the pricey room that he absolutely didn't need. He'd just wanted it. The smile curving her lush mouth was worth every hour he'd spent on the road with no other purpose than to get here and meet her when she got off the bus.

The drive to the hotel started in a taut silence. They both knew what was going on, and Adam understood that if he didn't focus on the road ahead, he was likely to throw the car into "Park" and pull onto the side of the freeway. It was only a question of whether or not they'd get arrested for some kind of public indecency. He thought they might be safer if he kept his mouth shut.

At last, the lingering space between them became too much and he opened his mouth in an effort to start a conversation that would get them all the way to the hotel. "How long are you home for?"

He might as well ask. After all, he'd already basically played his whole hand just in the way he showed up.

"Well, there's a week off of the tour."

His heart nearly crashed as his brain scrambled to figure out how he could spend the entire week in Nashville, but Hailey kept going. "However, the next three-week leg of the tour is going to be *Wilder*, not me."

Adam's chest expanded with sweet oxygen coming in along with the knowledge. Still, Hailey kept talking. Did she, like him, feel a need to fill the space with something other than reaching hands and ripped clothing?

"So I have four weeks before I go out again." She was still talking when he pulled up under the portico in front of the hotel. "And I'm very grateful for the break. I didn't think I would be, but Brenda was right."

He popped the trunk and grabbed her bag rather than letting the valet get it, though he did toss the keys to the man waiting at his door. Adam had grabbed Hailey's hand and didn't have one left for the ticket for his car, so she reached out and thanked the man, tucking the ticket into her pocket as though it was her own. It shouldn't have made his heart turn over like it did. She wasn't his. There wasn't a future for them here. But right now he didn't let that stop him.

It occurred to Adam as he tugged her up the steps and through the lobby, that he'd dreamed of this. Once. A long time ago.

He'd saved up his money and bought them a single night in the Days Inn outside of Kingston once. But this was lush and expensive and he took a moment to appreciate that he could afford to bring her here. She might be on stage, but he'd really "made it," even if it wasn't the way high school Adam had thought it would be.

It struck him then that he was very happy with the business. He'd sucked it up and told Jerry to buy the projectors, putting his payment plan back by a good margin. But as he pulled a warm and willing Hailey Watkins into the elevator with him, he breathed out a sigh that he'd done the right thing.

The rest of his life was right on track. Now if he could just figure out what to do with her...

Her eyes darted around the elevator and it took him a moment to realize she was checking for cameras. When she found none, she plunged her hands into his hair and pulled him close for a kiss that shot all his blood to his groin and sucked every thought from his brain.

By the time the elevator doors dinged, he had one hand on her ass under her skirt and the other down her shirt. He'd dropped her bag and his nice, silk t-shirt was shucked up under his arm as her hands roamed his chest.

Hailey Watkins was pressed into the railing along the side of the elevator as he looked into the hallway, grateful that it was empty. Then he grabbed her hand—almost forgot her bag—and tugged her down the hallway to his door.

24

Hailey sucked in a breath as she tumbled backward onto the hotel bed. It was plush and thick and she bounced a moment as Adam settled over her.

He felt *right* here, with her fingers in his hair and his hands tugging at her clothes. Her brain had been going non-stop for three weeks—thinking about being in public, which song was next on stage, keeping her "performing smile" in place all the time. But now, everything turned off except what she could feel. And Adam always made her feel amazing.

His focus said she was not only the only woman he saw, she might as well be the only one in the world. He *wanted* her. Other men wanted sex, and she fit the bill. Some of them wanted a girlfriend, someone to date or make their friends jealous. Sometimes, she'd fit that bill, too. But Adam didn't want something, he wanted *her*.

She gasped for air as he peeled the last of her clothing and began shucking what was left of his. The air was warm and charged around them even though he'd moved away and she missed the heat of him, even as it allowed her to look her fill.

The body in front of her was both new and familiar. She

knew the scar on his arm and how he'd gotten it. She knew the line of dark hair that directed her eye downward. The wide shoulders and muscles were new, as was the distinct cut of his jaw. It was no longer angular, but manly. He was no longer just tall; he'd lived up to his potential.

Her mouth watered. It was so easy to want him. So easy to forget the world around her. Tomorrow didn't matter. The tour didn't matter. She was here now and Adam was making her writhe.

Leaning over her again, he kept his fingers where they were, stroking her toward a climax. His mouth claimed hers, taking her sighs and gasps and almost-whimpers in a deep, needy kiss. Her breasts pressed against his bare chest and the contact felt almost cosmic, as though she and Adam, naked together, was the way the universe should be.

Though she was trying to hold back, Adam wasn't having it, and she was coming apart in his arms. Her fingernails dug into his biceps as she clung to him and let the sensation rock through her. Her head tipped back, her eyes glazed over, and her breath came in needy gasps.

Just as she began to come back to earth, she felt him move between her legs. *God, there was more.* There was always *more* with Adam. He pushed inside her as her ankles hooked behind him and her nails bit into his back, her greedy little heart beating harder.

He answered with sharp strokes letting her know he was close to his own edge. The intensity told her he wanted her to come again…and he could do it. He was the only one who'd ever taken the time to figure her out and apparently she still had the same triggers.

She called out his name, unable to stop it from flying from her lips as he practically growled with his own release, tumbling down on top of her. She stayed still for a moment, unable to move, spent and sated. Her open eyes would have been staring at the ceiling if she could see anything but sparkles floating in her vision.

Breathing heavily until the urge subsided, Hailey rolled over into Adam's arms as he lifted himself off. She was exhausted, but —in addition to having mind blowing sex—she'd been on the road for a long time. She sighed into darkness, grateful that the bed wasn't rumbling beneath her.

When she fully returned to her senses again, she stopped and savored the feeling of being in his arms for a moment. He wasn't asleep. She knew. This was earned knowledge of the man she was with.

Giving one more deep sigh, she let her head tip back, her heavy limbs spread across the cool sheets and almost laughed as her stomach growled.

"Hungry?" Adam grinned across the short space at her.

"Clearly."

"They've got twenty-four hour room service here," he said it with a grin, but she could feel her eyebrows raise.

"Part of your plan?" It seemed so convenient that he already knew.

His silence was more than an adequate answer.

So he intended to bring her here, make love to her into the night, and maybe even order room service. Or at least he'd been ready for that option. She had the option to say no, even if she didn't have the willpower. Still, Hailey wasn't sure how she felt about that.

She did like a man who could plan ahead. She wasn't sure if this was what she wanted him to plan for. Still, it irritated her a bit, even if she knew she had no grounds to be angry. Propping up on one elbow, she pushed the feelings aside and said, "Well then, let's see what they'll deliver at three a.m."

Five minutes later, he was sitting naked, cross-legged on the bed staring at her as they looked through the menu. "All these options, and you want *oatmeal*?"

"Oh, God. Yes," Hailey replied. The sound of her voice might be as drenched in desire as it had been while they've been making love. "Do you know what we ate on the road? Nothing healthy. Oatmeal sounds so good right now. And look, a side of peaches and blueberries. Fresh fruit!"

"You didn't get fresh fruit on the road? That seems inhumane."

"Well," she shrugged. They'd been offered fruit as some road-side dives and the gas stations they passed had little plastic containers of grapes and cheese or the occasional banana, but none of it had been enticing. "The *fresh* part was questionable a lot of the time."

Adam quirked one side of his mouth and proceeded to order her a very expensive bowl of oatmeal. He, however, didn't hold anything back and ordered steak, eggs, hash browns and more.

But after the call was in, it didn't seem there was much more to say. Hailey began wondering if he really was just her friend with benefits—less emphasis on the "Friend" part. It was what she'd agreed to but, sitting in the hotel with him at three in the morning, the idea had lost some of its shine. She was opening her mouth, unable to stand the silence any longer and not knowing if he really wanted to talk to her or not, when his words cut her off.

"I missed you while you were gone."

"Really?" The admission startled her and she wasn't able to stop her stunned question before it tumbled out. She wished she had clothing on, because suddenly she felt naked. "You missed me? But what did you miss?"

Why did she ask hard questions? This was supposed to be an easy relationship—if it was a relationship at all. Wasn't it more of a handshake agreement and great sex? But she'd chucked her question into the space between them and now she had the uncomfortable task of waiting for the answer.

25

Adam felt her words almost like a punch to the gut. *She didn't believe him.*

He'd missed her so much, and she sat there as though he was lying just to have something to say.

They'd never had a chasm like this between them before, but it had been so long, maybe they weren't *them* anymore. Though he thought that through logically, he couldn't make the feeling of having been socked disappear. "I don't understand."

He didn't. What had been easy, and sexy, and fun was suddenly difficult. Awkward.

Hailey didn't seem to have problems though. Her tone wasn't dreamy or wishful; it had sharp edges that he tried to back away from. "What exactly did you miss about me, Adam?"

He understood she meant it. But her saying practically the same thing again didn't really clarify what she wanted from him. Still, he *tried*. "I missed the sound of your voice. I missed seeing your texts in the middle of the afternoon. I missed..."

What else was there to say?

Just when he was about to open his mouth, her words flowed into the air between them.

"You missed sleeping with me?" Though the words themselves were polite, the question reeked of accusation. It was a rough question from a woman who'd suggested they could be friends with benefits and that it would be fine. Clearly, something about it was not. But if there was one thing he'd learned before, being less than honest wouldn't get him anywhere.

"Sure, that too." But even as he said the three short words, he knew they were the wrong ones. Instantly, he felt himself begin to backpedal and try to defend what he'd said. "Isn't that what we agreed on? We're exclusive and we're having sex. Right?"

"It is." Her voice and her tone were agreeable. The clipped nature of the words wasn't. He knew there was something more and he tried to be patient. What he got back instead was, "I guess I missed you, too."

It didn't sound like the declaration he'd hoped for. He'd missed her, badly. Hell, he'd missed her for eight long years, but he was pretty sure that wasn't the right thing to say either. So he tried one last time. "I miss talking to you. I missed hearing how your day went. I missed…"

Just then, he paused, unsure if he was going to play this card. It felt big, but then he thought, *What the hell!* She couldn't break his heart as badly as she had the last time. *Could she?* "I miss knowing that, at the end of the day, you are still mine."

He heard the words only after they were out. He heard that it sounded angry, but it was too late and there was nothing he could do about it. Besides, she was the one who started this conversation. They had been having a good time. In fact, there was going to be a knock on the door from room service at any moment, and what should have been a happy, go-lucky scene was now filled with terse words.

He let it all sit for a minute while Hailey visibly absorbed what he said. He could tell she was making decisions about how to respond. If he was betting on the outcome, he'd put his money on "wouldn't like what he got."

"The thing is Adam…"

Yeah, he shouldn't have played that last card.

"—I don't know how you missed hearing my voice when mostly you texted me. And I don't know how you missed hearing about my day, when we never talked about it. And I don't know how you missed knowing that I'm yours at the end of the night. I don't think you're mine or I'm yours. We had a pretty clear agreement. But you're right that I shouldn't have asked."

"That is what we agreed. I agreed to it too, but I don't know that I still want that." They'd had all of three rendezvous between them, and he was already failing miserably. He was failing at the rest of it, too, since it didn't seem he could stop his mouth from confessing everything. He was handing her every tool she needed to break him, but he just kept going. "It's just that we used to talk about everything. Now it's only about sex. I guess that's a harder adjustment for me than I thought it was going to be."

He was failing at "keeping it light." This was not the way friends-with-benefits was supposed to go. He'd had a friend with benefits once, and she'd told him she found someone new and Adam had just wished her luck. With Hailey? Even this conversation—where she wasn't leaving him…yet—everything felt like a punch to the gut.

Sure enough, the knock came at the door right then and neither of them had any clothes on.

Popping up, Adam motioned for her to step into the bathroom, where she could at least hide from the hotel employees. Calling out for them to wait, he hopped around for a moment as he pulled on pants and a T shirt before inviting the server in. A beautiful table was carefully set in the middle of the tiny space in the hotel room.

Well, Adam thought, *the food was prettier than their relationship right now.*

When they were alone again, he knocked on the bathroom door and was surprised when Hailey emerged dressed. But then he realized that she'd pulled on a pair of her own jeans, but she was in one of his shirts. It took him a moment to place how she'd gotten it. He'd ducked into the hotel, gotten his room key and even changed after the drive in from Knoxville before heading down to the Heart Beats parking lot to meet her. He must have left the shirt in the bathroom.

And here was Hailey, just like old times, looking like she was his.

It hit him hard as he stared at her. Maybe he didn't miss hearing her voice or hearing her talking about her day—not recently—because they hadn't been doing that. She was right. But he did miss those things. Maybe missing her wasn't something new. He'd missed all of her for so long already.

After laying so many of his cards on the table tonight, he decided to hold that one closer to the chest. So instead of telling her, he did the second dumbest thing he could do. He reached out, took her hand and pulled her over to the table. Playing the gentleman, he pulled out her chair for her as though they were in their prom gown and tux rather than the discarded clothing they'd scooped off the hotel room floor. Once he was seated, he said, "You're right. We're not doing those things. We don't talk enough, and we don't tell each other about our days. And yet, somehow, I still miss them."

He paused, but Hailey just looked at him with those big blue eyes he knew so, so well. This would be up to him, so he put it out there.

"Do you want to be something more?"

26

Hailey woke up at midnight, in her own apartment, under her own fluffy comforter. Alone.

There was no cat to curl at her feet or greet her at the door. But she'd known that would be the case. There was also no Adam sleeping beside her, not like he'd been last night. For today, she thought that was probably a good thing. Even if it didn't feel as good as having him curled up next to her did.

They'd asked each other some hard questions, which was her own fault. She had herself a good setup with Adam. She had a friend with benefits that she trusted. But she'd gone and gotten angry about him doing exactly what she told him to.

Not very mature, she chastised herself as she rolled over, tangling the covers around herself.

He'd asked if she wanted them to be something more to each other and she'd told him she didn't know.

It wasn't a lie. She *didn't* know if she wanted to be something more. That it was the truth didn't change the fact that it was a shitty answer. On the one hand, she did want more. She missed him, too, despite the fact that everything she said was true. They *didn't* talk. But she understood what he meant: she missed hearing his voice, too. She'd told him she didn't know, because she wasn't sure if following her feelings headlong down this steep hill was the right thing to do. It certainly didn't seem the *smart* thing to do.

At least he'd let her non-answer stand. "Then we go on as we are, and if you find you want to change things, let me know."

It was all he'd said as they finished their middle-of-the-night breakfast, crawled back into bed, and curled into each other's arms. She'd been falling asleep when he reached for her again.

This time, when they made love, it was slow and sweet. Hailey felt as if she was making promises with her body that her brain and her heart wouldn't quite commit to. Was Adam doing the same thing?

It *felt* like he was, but she couldn't be certain.

After, when they fell into a deep sleep, their limbs were entangled and she could feel their hearts beating next to each other, almost as though they really meant it this time. But she'd woken abruptly to the harsh mechanical beeping of his phone.

He'd smacked it off and rolled back into her, but Hailey had already asked what it was for.

"Checkout time is eleven." He'd mumbled it into her hair, already falling back asleep even as he volunteered to pay for the extra day at the hotel.

It was Hailey who wasn't sure if she could handle it. So she told him she had to leave. She said she had a meeting, and she was pretty sure he saw right through the lie.

In fact, the only meeting she had was her head meeting this pillow in this bed.

She'd slept all through today and on into the middle of the night, when she finally woke up. After a few minutes, she found herself standing over her stove in her underwear. Still groggy from twisting her schedule and her heart into knots, she scrambled an egg from the carton she'd picked up after he dropped her at the apartment.

She'd gone on long trips before, left her place empty for several weeks at a time. But she couldn't remember the last time it had felt quite so cold coming back. The place had been stale and empty and musty.

She'd been smart enough to turn right around after Adam dropped her off. Freshly showered and with her hair up in a ponytail, Hailey had headed straight for the grocery store.

Even though she'd snagged a few essentials, her food supplies were lower than usual. She'd eaten everything perishable before she left. Now, she looked around wondering what else she could make to eat. In one cupboard a small blue box of cornbread mix caught her eye. She only needed one egg and some water.

The mix was in the bowl and the egg cracked before she realized she didn't have any bottled water. For a moment she ran the tap and contemplated using the city water, but the tap never ran quite clear enough for her. It was why she always—well, *almost* always—had bottled water in the fridge.

Then she reached into her suitcase. *Hell*, she thought, *she'd already drunk the True Springs fountain water*. She might as well make Mabel happy and use it. Surely there was a half cup in there. She eyeballed the jar, opened it and sniffed.

It certainly looked clearer than what the sink was providing. Hailey scowled at it. Was it really from the fountain? Had it been in there with the pennies and nickels and whatever else the town children threw in? The water in the jar looked far too clear. It was probably just filtered tap water from True Springs. Mabel likely sold these for cash, wishing each person luck from their adorable little Mason jar as she pocketed the change...not that she'd asked for any from Hailey.

Whatever. If anything about the town name was accurate, then this had to be better than what was coming through her pipes in East Nashville. She dumped the water into the bowl and stirred, reminding herself that she didn't believe it, so it didn't matter anyway.

Mabel had already slipped her some fountain water in her cocoa earlier. So if it was going to have any effect, wouldn't she have seen it already?

Hailey contemplated that as she stirred, then poured the batter into little paper cups in her cupcake tin. She popped the whole thing into the oven, still wondering if she'd done something ridiculous. But then she thought back to last night, to how she'd felt, how she and Adam had stared at each other, not knowing what to say or do if they weren't having sex. If True Springs, fountain water was the miracle the town claimed, last night should have gone dramatically differently.

Clearly, it was all a hoax to bring in tourists. Hailey added "bottled water" to her growing grocery list and waited for the timer to ding.

27

Hailey was trying and Adam had to give her credit for that, he thought as she asked him, "So did you buy the projectors?"

She looked up at him from where she stood at the stove.

"I did. I bit the bullet. It was a lot of money." It was the kind of money neither of them had ever expected to see. At least not until Hailey made it big. He laughed. "I don't have that kind of money just sitting in my pockets. The debt on the business is huge."

Hailey nodded and stirred the chili she was heating up for them. She had invited him over for dinner and that was a first. He'd accepted, thinking it was almost like a first date, but it had been difficult not to pounce on her when she opened the door. His only effort of restraint was to give her a deep kiss and step quickly away.

He was going to do this, he told himself, *they* could do this. So he hung back, set the table, and watched her stir chili and heat corn bread. It wasn't anything fancy. Hailey was no great cook, but it meant more to him that she was doing the work than if they just ordered out somewhere. So he could try to stick to his part—his part was keeping his hands and his tongue to himself.

"I think if you look at the finances of the company, you would think I'm a lot better off than I am. Right now, it's running more like a farm where there's a lot of money that goes through, but not much actually filtering into my hands."

She smiled at him. "But you've got your own place now."

"An apartment. Yes. It's in a nice building." Then he went and said another dumb thing. Just threw it out there like he'd thrown out the dumb thing last time. Well, maybe it was paying off? "You could come up and see my place. Hang out on my patio and watch the fog settle into the mountains. Enjoy Knoxville. Maybe you can think up a new song." Adam threw the last part in there, as though he could save face by suggesting his overly-lyrical invite would be 'work' for her.

At least she said, "That's a good idea," as though she would actually consider it.

Maybe miracles did happen.

Hailey stopped stirring and began to serve the chili with Fritos, onions, black olives, sour cream and grated cheese. She placed a little basket of cornbread in the middle of the table. He'd considered bringing a bottle of wine but was glad he'd brought beer instead.

As Adam dug in the first bite hit his tongue, impressing him. "Oh, this is good." He realized this clearly wasn't the same recipe she'd been using in high school. Things had changed, and he needed to keep that memory firmly planted at the front of his mind. He tried to pull the conversation along. "What about you? What did you do in the last three days?"

"Let's see... I wrote a new song. I reworked an old song and did headshots."

"Do you still need headshots? I thought those were for auditions."

"Nope. I don't think I ever get to quit doing headshots. As

much as I would like to." She chewed for a moment, then went on. "We do them for advertising and posters. Sometimes they'll use a head shot on a demo."

"They should put one on the side of your bus," he offered, thinking it was a good idea. Instead his suggestion was met with laughter and an exaggerated roll of her eyes.

"If only. My bus is as plain as the day is long. No headshot on the side for me."

He picked up one of the corn breads, peeled the cupcake paper off and cracked it in half. Only, as he buttered it and stuck half of it into his mouth at once, Hailey looked at him with a slightly odd glint in her eye. Hailey moved on to a new subject before he could ask, changing the topic fast enough to make his head spin.

"So, what's this Hilton gig you keep talking about?" She posed the question as she leaned forward and took several dainty bites, as if one could be dainty while eating chili.

This new Hailey was slightly more refined than the older one, as though she'd been trained to wink for the camera and always have that megawatt smile ready for everyone. But underneath, she was still *his Hailey*. And wasn't that the problem? *His Hailey* had packed up and left him the last time.

Maybe she'd never been his. Maybe it was all his mistake. Adam quickly finished the other half of the cornbread and told her how this new job would take his company all over the country. "I'm renting trucks. That's a big expense. I don't own the trucks yet."

"So, once you get the projectors paid off, you get to buy trucks? Is it one of those businesses?" She took a bite of her own cornbread, though she didn't shove half of it in her mouth at once. "One where the technology always changes and you're constantly upgrading and spending money."

"Pretty much."

She'd hit the nail on the head and summed up why he was up to his ears in mortgages and loans. "Do you ever earn it back?"

"Oh, absolutely. Right now, it's the debt of buying the company that's the biggest cost. The pieces rent out for far more than the payments. In the end, you can sell off your old tech for even more profit. If you do it at the right time."

"Interesting." She shook her head and he wanted to ask *what?* But she answered before he could get the words out. "This just isn't where I thought you would wind up. It suits you, though. You look good as a company owner—as the boss man."

Adam couldn't help but smile. But, right then, his phone chimed. For a moment, he entertained the thought that he shouldn't look at it. He was at dinner with Hailey. But maybe he should keep things casual. So he pulled the phone out and checked the screen.

As soon as he did it, he wished he hadn't. It was a message from his mother.

– Come tomorrow. I've got news.

Given that the last time she'd said she had news for him, she's had cancer, it wasn't surprising that his stomach twisted into a cold hard knot.

28

"What?" Hailey asked as she felt concern wash through her.

Adam had looked at his phone briefly. He'd been smiling when he pulled it out but, in a heartbeat, everything about him shifted.

She pushed again, "What's wrong?"

Adam only shook his head, as if to say he didn't want to talk about it. But wasn't that the whole point of cooking him chili and keeping her hands to herself? He'd asked if she wanted to be something more but now—when it counted—he was holding back. Suddenly, even though she knew he was upset about what he'd seen, she was angry.

"You asked if I wanted to be something more, I was trying. But maybe what we have isn't anything more than this and never will be. Not again."

As she spoke, the color drained from his face, but she was already going like a little steamroller. Her inertia carried her forward and she was unable to stop. "I can make you dinner. You can take me out. But if you don't tell me what's going on, then there's no forward to go to. So, don't ask again."

Unable to deal with the cold look in his eyes, Hailey smacked her silverware down onto the table and stood up as though she was going to go grab another beer. Mostly, she was just standing up and walking away because she needed to.

"It's my mother," he finally said.

That didn't tell her much of anything. She'd already known he had a mother, but at least it was a start. Turning around, Hailey leaned against the bar that led to her tiny kitchen and waited. This was going to be up to him how things would go down.

Eventually Adam took a deep breath and added, "She said she has news."

When he didn't elaborate, Hailey began to prod though maybe she should have dropped it. Once she got started, it became clear that had been the wrong move, but she was already on a roll. "Come on. That's all? Obviously, that's *not* everything. That might be everything she wrote in the text, but that's not enough to make you turn white as a ghost."

He nodded then, as though catching on that she was going to push until either he told her or she broke him apart. For whatever reason there was an immense satisfaction in knowing that she was done pussyfooting around. "Tell me Adam. Or leave."

Very carefully, he set his hands at the edge of the table as though he needed to anchor himself to the place. He stayed perfectly still. "The last time she used those words, she had cancer."

Hailey frowned. "What do you mean *she had cancer*?"

This time, Adam at least moved, his expression changed until he no longer looked cold and petrified. Now, he looked confused. "What do you mean? You *know* she had cancer. She found the lump right before you left."

"No, she *didn't* have cancer," Hailey added, her conviction bumping up against his confusion. Strange swirly sensations formed in her lungs as she slowly breathed in and out. Mrs. Zucker had *not* had cancer.

His mother had been doing what she always did: making up anything she could to throw a wedge between her son and the girlfriend she didn't like. Hailey had a few moments of his silence to put everything together. "Is that what she told you?"

"What do you mean *what she told me*, Hailey?" He started to rise from his seat. Stepping away, he paced the tiny space of her apartment almost running into the coffee table the area was so tiny. But he kept walking anyway, his angry footfalls surely bothering her downstairs neighbors. "She had *cancer*, Hailey. The lump that she found—it was malignant."

The swirls in her lungs stopped, maybe because her breathing stopped. Again? They were doing this same thing *again*? This was the exact same problem as their first time around. She'd left him in her dust because he'd chosen his manipulative mother over her. He'd chosen the woman who lied to get her way. His mother had done everything she could to end their relationship.

Mrs. Zucker had consistently told Adam that Hailey trying to be a country star was the stupidest thing she'd ever heard. She'd even spoken the words out loud on more than one occasion, that Hailey's dreams were going to drag them both down and ruin Adam's life. Adam had always told her no, that he didn't believe that. He told his mother that he loved Hailey, but when the time came? He always sided with his family.

And, dammit, Hailey was supposed to be his family. But he hadn't come with her, had he? Now, he was doing it again: believing his mother instead of her. Hailey could feel everything inside her freeze up and it was probably better than feeling the sharp stab of pain at his words.

Hailey didn't say any of what she was thinking. Instead, she turned her head a little to the side. His family had always been a sore spot between them. His father had been reluctantly accepting, apparently thinking that Adam would simply grow out of a childhood relationship. His mother hadn't forbade them from seeing each other, but she'd sabotaged them every chance she'd gotten and, obviously, eventually succeeded.

So Hailey put the words on her tongue. "I hate to ask this—" She really did. Not because she didn't believe it, but she didn't want to hear him say that she was wrong, that he still believed his mother. "Did you see it?"

"Did I see her cancer?" He sounded as if she'd asked him if he'd watched the surgery happen or seen the cells themselves.

She almost blurted out "Yes!" but she managed to keep at least that in check. "No. Did you see her going to chemotherapy? Not just leaving house, but actually getting hooked up to IVs in the hospital? Did you talk to her doctor or see a report or something?"

Her hands were waving wildly now, her distress showing through as it occurred to her for the first time in eight years that she might have been very, very wrong.

29

"Yes."

Adam's single word hit her like a cold gust of wind, and Hailey froze where she stood. His mother had actually had cancer? That was a question she should never have had to ask, but she didn't trust Mrs. Zucker any further than she could throw the woman.

This time it was Adam who stopped and stared at her in disbelief. "Did you really not believe she had cancer?"

"No. I didn't."

"How could you not believe me when I said that?"

Hailey shook her head. She felt awful now for denying that someone had cancer, but at the time? There had been no other decision to make. How could she explain to Adam now that nothing Mrs. Zucker said had ever been true? Why would that one thing have been right?

She tried to explain. "Adam, it's not that I didn't believe *you*. It's that I didn't believe *her*. She thought I was terrible. She thought that I was going to ruin your life. Your mother would have done anything to break us up."

He blinked, his eyes growing wider as his expression somehow grew even more disbelieving. "You thought she *made up cancer?*"

"Yes." Hailey wanted the word to be forceful, but it came out more like a whisper, more like a question.

Adam's frown only grew deeper until he finally spoke. "I guess I never really knew you at all." With a stiffness setting in across his shoulders, he started for the door.

"No!" She yelled it at him. "No! You don't get to walk out in the middle of this. I told you this *last time.* When your mother first announced that she thought she had cancer, I *told you* that I didn't believe her. And I told you *why.* But you walked out."

She sucked in a breath but didn't let it stop her. "That's why we broke up. That's why I left. Because you wouldn't talk to me."

At least that made him pause. His hand was already on the doorknob, not quite opening it yet. Instead, he turned around. "Hailey, there was nothing to talk about. You had already decided that you were leaving. You also decided that whatever happened to me didn't matter. You couldn't wait just six months or a year for me to take care of my family."

She yelled at him now. *"There was no family to take care of! She wasn't sick!"*

Hailey heard her voice bouncing off the four walls and wondered what her neighbors must think. Usually, she was quiet. She didn't have a pet. She didn't throw parties. Occasionally, she played her guitar late at night and the neighbors knocked on their ceiling and the walls at her then. What must they be thinking about this?

Right then, she knew she was making a critical decision. She could tell him that he had been right all those years ago, that nothing would have stopped her. Or she could let him walk out the door again not knowing what she really thought.

If she let him go, it would be over. She would never ever see him again. He would become a stranger that she had once loved very, very much. Her other option was to plant her feet and stand and fight. The difference with fighting was that she didn't know the outcome.

Hailey threw her first real punch. "That woman made up everything."

She knew Adam didn't like it when she referred to his mother as *that woman*. But, right now, she couldn't find anything more gracious to say.

"Hailey…"

"We've had this fight before. Do you remember?" She almost laughed. "It was a long time ago, and you didn't believe me then. But right now, you get to re-decide if you do. You did *not* have a family emergency on homecoming. Your little sister was *not* in the ER."

Adam shook his head as though shaking off something that didn't agree with him. "What are you talking about?"

There had been so many family emergencies. Babysitters that didn't show up. Car problems. Late nights at work. All things that Mrs. Zucker called on Adam to fix—all things that interfered with time he'd planned with Hailey. He'd constantly canceled on her, and she'd let him. But they'd missed homecoming because of an emergency room visit for Chelsea.

Adam was still shaking his head. "Chelsea was sick. She needed an IV. She was in the hospital until the middle of the night."

"No, she wasn't." Hailey was proud of her calm voice. It had all been a lie, but her evidence was a gamble. "Call her. Call Chelsea right now. Ask your sister, not your mother—because your mother will just lie to you again. But ask your sister if she'll tell you the truth now that she's an adult. Ask if she was actually sick, if she was actually even in the emergency room that night."

Hailey had to hope that would be enough. She had to hope that his little sister had grown up enough to tell the truth. Or maybe she hadn't figured out that Adam was seeing Hailey again and might think it didn't matter.

Adam only stared at her while he pulled out his phone and dialed.

Great, she thought. It was probably going to take three days for Chelsea to reply and *hopefully* tell him the truth. Hailey's confidence faltered. Whatever Mrs. Zucker said at the time convinced her daughters to lie, too. Adam had bought the story, hook, line and sinker. But maybe there was hope this time. Hailey held her breath while she watched him wait for an answer.

"Hey, Chelse," he said, startling Hailey. His sister had actually picked up the line! So she listened while he asked random questions and eventually said, "Thank you" before hanging up. He'd said "yes," a handful of times in between, but Hailey didn't know what it meant. So she waited with her heart in her throat for him to speak.

Adam took a slow deep breath, it looked like he was centering himself, but Hailey *knew* him. His changed expression meant that Chelsea had finally recanted her story of a stomach bug that had sent her into the ER and canceled the all-night party the teenaged Hailey and Adam had planned.

He didn't even say that Chelsea had finally told him the truth. He didn't have to. Instead, his shoulders slumped as he asked, "You never believed her? I guess you were right about *that one*. But why do you still think she lied about *everything*?"

Hailey tossed her head back and forth for a moment. "Do you want the truth?"

"Always."

She didn't quite believe that. He'd not listened to the truth in the past, but if she was fighting for this, she would try again. "Your mother liked to corner me when you weren't around. She liked to tell me how she was going to break us up, and how you would never leave your family behind. Certainly, not for me. She told me to my face that you wouldn't come with me and that I didn't stand a chance against her."

Hailey laughed at the cold, bitter memories. When the feeling finally drained out of her system, she crossed her arms and looked up at him. "I told her she was wrong, that I didn't believe she could do it. I didn't think anything could break us up. But you know what? In the end, she was right."

30

A dam still couldn't breathe. His hands wrapped tightly around the steering wheel, gripping it with far more force than was necessary. He had left Hailey standing in the middle of her apartment, with dinner still sitting on the table—half eaten. She'd stared at him as he walked out.

He shouldn't have left like that, but between what Chelsea had admitted, and what Hailey told him, he hadn't been able to process the new information at all.

He'd gotten himself a hotel room when he first came into town this evening. In his mind, he was being a good citizen. He was only *dating* Hailey, not expecting to spend the night. The hotel was proof that he was as good as his word. But, now, when he was trying to flee town, he had to go back and get his things.

Pulling up under the low, slightly sagging overhang, he counted the silver numbers tacked to each orange door. This time, he was staying in cheap digs. Though he was proud that he could afford the nice hotel for Hailey the week before, it wasn't something he could afford to do every time.

He hadn't been lying about the business operating with tight margins. Though he wouldn't admit to it at work, he ate ramen noodles or cereal for dinner more evenings than was healthy. Any way he could squeeze every last penny into the business.

Grabbing everything, Adam left the key on the dresser, before throwing his bag haphazardly into the back seat. His Mercedes buzzed down the street giving a good kick of speed. The car was an expense he'd accepted for the image at work—like eating decent lunches but cheap dinners. He didn't tell people he'd gotten the car secondhand.

The car swerved to miss the small silver hatchback in the next lane as it tried to pull over on him. He hadn't seen it, he'd been so focused, so angry and confused. Before he made it to his mother's he'd almost changed lanes right on top of someone twice.

Hailey was right. He said it to himself again. *Hailey was right.*

Though he'd always known his mother didn't like his girl-friend, he hadn't believed it was as bad as Hailey had always complained. Until tonight, he hadn't even entertained the possi-bility that it was anything more than Hailey being young and self-centered.

But now he looked back and tried to drag it all up. His mother had told him repeatedly that *Hailey wasn't right for him.* Occasion-ally, she'd even enlisted his father to say so as well. Though the old man had been reluctant to join in, he'd added his two cents from time to time. Still, Adam never imagined that his mother had actively maneuvered the situation to drive them apart.

Hell, he hadn't even believed she'd said so directly to Hailey's face.

His breath huffed out into a harsh sigh inside the car. The driveway bumped underneath him, the old gravel needing to be raked again. Normally, he would have filed that away, picked a date to come back and do the job for her. Now, he thought about what else his mother might have lied about. She'd done it at least once.

His mother wasn't content just doing these things herself; she'd enlisted his little sister to help stop his homecoming date.

Jesus.

Suddenly, he was questioning everything. All the times that he and Hailey had been interrupted. All the times his mother had suddenly *needed* something and he'd had to cancel at the last minute. It seemed normal back then: just the way families ran. It made sense that he was really the only one who got interrupted. He was the oldest. If his parents had to leave, it was logical that he would stay home to babysit. It all made sense at the time. But was any of it real?

He smacked his hands against the steering wheel.

In high school, Hailey had been very good natured about all the times his family had interfered. As teenagers living under their parents' roofs, Adam figured it was to be expected. Her family didn't interfere because she didn't really have a family. If her mother had a new boyfriend in the trailer or if there was a fight, Hailey would retreat to her bedroom. After closing the door, she would simply drop out the window. No one had ever missed her.

It hit him then. A ton of bricks weighing down his heart with sudden comprehension. Hailey hadn't understood his need to stay behind for his family—because she hadn't understood *family*. He wasn't sure if she was even in touch with her mother now. He'd always wondered if something had happened to Hailey, if her mother would even bother to report her missing. Mrs. Pulaski wasn't abusive—at least not as far as Adam had ever known—but she was neglectful enough that he'd always been surprised that Hailey was such an amazing person.

So he sat in the driveway for a moment and got himself together before confronting his mother about what she'd done. All of this had been triggered by the text that said she had news.

And no good had ever come of that.

31

Hailey stood, stunned, for a full minute. She looked at the four walls around her as though Adam should be there. He should at least be frowning at her, maybe be angry. But he'd just walked out.

When she finally got herself together, Hailey cleaned up their interrupted dinner. Picking up half-eaten bowls of chili, she consoled herself with a task she could complete. Obviously, she was a failure at love, but she could clear the table.

She scraped the food Adam had left behind down the garbage disposal and set her own bowl aside. She would likely get hungry later, since she hadn't really eaten anything. The pit in her stomach made her wonder when that would be. Still, she pulled out plastic wrap and covered the food, then put it in the fridge with rote motions.

Next she plucked the basket off the table. She'd lined it with a checkered napkin and filled it with the remaining cornbread muffins. For a moment, she thought about putting them away too. *Screw it*, she thought. *They were worthless.*

Fountain water that finds your true love was probably the

dumbest thing she'd ever heard. True springs had a racket going and nothing more. She should never have believed that it worked. Taking the muffins to the trash, she flipped her wrist and dumped the remaining ones inside. They made satisfying sounds as they hit the bottom of the bag.

She still wasn't sure what had triggered Adam to walk out the door. He'd fooled her. He'd had his hand on the knob and she'd accused him of leaving in the middle of every fight. But, this time, he'd turned around and stayed even though he was mad, even though she was yelling. Her heart had soared. He had *stayed.*

But sure enough, it hadn't lasted very long. The second time, there hadn't been a pause. No warning at all. He'd simply been out the door before she'd really even realized he was leaving.

So here she was, just like last time. She told herself, everything was the same as it was before she'd seen Adam again. Aside from the tour that she'd gone on—which she'd done without Adam—nothing was really different from a month and a half ago.

Yet, everything was. What had been normal now felt like a gaping hole. She and Adam had tried to be friends with benefits. They'd managed to upgrade, just a little bit, to lovers. But when they tried to be something more, once again, everything had fallen apart.

She was still stunned that his mother had actually had cancer. After all the lies and the manipulation, Hailey had felt smart catching on that the opportune diagnosis was just something Mrs. Zucker had made up to keep Adam from leaving. That her assumption—one she'd been so certain of—had been wrong hurt her heart. She wouldn't have asked Adam to leave his mother if she'd been sick, but Hailey had never believed it was true.

That didn't change anything now though. She couldn't change the past, and she couldn't change that Adam had gone out the door again.

For the last time, she gritted her teeth and tried to find a way to be okay. Given that they tried this again as grown ups, and that it had blown up on them again, maybe it was best that it happened the way it did. At least that's what she told herself. As she picked up her guitar, she played a few notes and felt like crap.

So she wrote and wrote and poured her heart out. While she cried, she sang that maybe things happened for a reason.

32

"Is it cancer?" Adam asked in a tone that was harsher than he intended.

He'd walked in the front door, seen his mother, and hugged her hard. But these were his first words. He didn't add that he wasn't just questioning the news she'd messaged about, but her integrity as well. He let the question hang between them as he looked in her eyes and wished he could tell what she was thinking.

She looked at him for a moment as though making a decision. Then she nodded. This time, given the stunning information he just learned from Hailey, Adam took a different tack than he would have otherwise. Certainly, a different one than he'd taken the first time. "Where's the report from the doctor?"

He'd tried to ask it as though he simply wanted medical information rather than insinuating that he didn't believe her.

His mother looked startled. Probably that was a reasonable reaction as this was the first time he'd asked for any paperwork. "I don't have it."

"Surely it's online. Maybe in an email the doctor's office sent. Let's look it up." He probably wasn't doing a very good job of being subtle. The way his mother had responded, he'd clearly veered outside of his norm.

"I don't know," she said, her head pulling back as though he were advancing on her. "I don't have a way to get it. How about I call the doctor's office next week and get them to send it?"

Not good enough, Adam thought ungraciously. It would take more than that to pull the wool over his eyes this time. He was shocked at how much his position had changed. If Hailey hadn't told him what she had…if she hadn't made him call Chelsea…he would have hugged his mother and worried. Now he analyzed her every move.

She sat down on the couch and Adam took the chair, the coffee table marking the space between them. This time, he merely stared at her for a moment, trying to make his decisions. The three-hour drive had not been long enough to sort out all of his feelings.

She began fidgeting, plucking the crocheted Afghan thrown over the back of the couch as though she were nervous. *Why would she be nervous?* he thought, *Unless....*

"The doctor said he wants me to start chemo in two weeks."

"I'll go with you. I'll keep you company while you have your treatments." Adam immediately volunteered. So he would know she'd actually spent the time hooked up to medication this time.

"Oh, I don't need you to do that." She waved him away, then added, "Just drop me off and pick me up."

That was what he'd done the last time. He tried to remember, had she looked sicker or weaker at the end? Or did she merely spent two hours running around the hospital? The possibility bothered him deep into his core. Had he even seen the medical bills? Or had he just sent money?

He could wait a week and go to a doctor's appointment with her. He could talk to the doctor himself. That would be enough proof, he thought, but he didn't want to wait a week or two or three.

It only occurred to him, as he sat there in his old living room with his mother, that he'd completely walked out on Hailey. He'd been so stunned and so confused and so suddenly in need of answers from his mother that his body had merely popped up and headed off to get them.

Shit.

Ignoring his mother for a moment, he pulled out his phone and wrote out a short message.

— I'm sorry. Didn't mean to just leave. Sitting with my mother getting answers.

It wasn't much of an apology, he realized. But he wasn't sure what else to say until he actually had the answers he needed.

What he expected was to have his mother suggest that Hailey was the liar here. But as he thought that through, he remembered Chelsea had confirmed it. She'd never gone to the ER. Their mother had taken her out for pizza.

"Is that work?" His mother asked pointing to his phone.

It was a prime opportunity, and he took it. "No, mom. I'm messaging Hailey."

His mother's eyes narrowed, but she didn't look surprised.

What the fuck? he thought. He hadn't seen Hailey in years. Why wouldn't his mother be shocked that he was suddenly speaking to his ex? Unless she already knew that he was seeing Hailey. If she did, well that made the sudden recurrence of her cancer way too convenient.

Would she really do that? Would she really put her kid through a fake cancer diagnosis over a girlfriend she didn't like? Adam took a deep breath. It was time to get real answers.

"Mom, there are several things I need to know. And I need you to answer honestly."

33

"Oh my god, Adam, how could you accuse me of such a thing?" His mother was angry and startled and she was willing to let him see that.

Apparently, she was finally beginning to feel the same way he was. "I really have cancer, I can't believe—"

He waved a hand to cut her off. "You want to know how I could accuse you of this? Well, let's just talk about the fact that the timing is really fishy. It's been eight years since I've seen Hailey. But I found her and we're together again. And suddenly, you've got the same problem that broke us up in the first place."

She looked appalled and even laid her hand on her chest. "You think I got cancer to break you up?"

All Adam could do was shrug, as if to say, *maybe you did*.

"How can you accuse me of such a thing?"

Maybe it was time to answer, because he finally believed he was starting to see things more clearly. "Well, this time, Hailey didn't leave for Nashville and walk out my door. Instead, she tried again to tell me about all the times you'd confronted her. How you told her that you were never going to let us be together."

He stopped there, but he could see his mother processing his words. She wasn't shocked or offended. She was calculating! Even though she held very, very, very still, he could see the twitch in her.

Holy crap! It was true. Sure, he'd already corroborated part of the story, but some stupid part of him had held out hope there was a decent explanation. There wasn't. His mother had actually cornered Hailey at least once and she clearly remembered doing it. His voice was low and thrumming with his building anger. "I can't believe you would do that to me, mom."

"She was never right for you." From her expression, his mother didn't even regret doing it. "I told you that and I told her that, too. *So sue me.*"

The defensive edge to his mother's voice was something he wasn't used to hearing. Hailey had always accused Mrs. Zucker of being manipulative. Adam had never really believed her; he'd always just let the accusations roll off as though they were Hailey's problem. *Dear God, he'd wronged Hailey in so many ways.*

Hailey had been right all along. His mother cajoled, whined, and threw guilt around like she was making a Jackson Pollock painting. But this was new.

"There's no crime in telling you or her what I thought. And I was *right*. She left you." After a righteous sniff, his mother continued. Not with any apology but with full out defense of what she'd done. "You would never have that company if that girl had stayed around."

"No," he said. "You are right about that. But I might have had *Hailey*."

The press of his mother's lips let him know exactly how much his mother thought his girlfriend weighed against this company. He'd always known his mother wasn't in favor of the relationship, but apparently she'd actively tried to sabotage it.

She plucked at the Afghan again, only this time her lips

pursed. "Look, just because I didn't like your girlfriend is no reason to accuse me of faking cancer."

"That's true." Adam let the words sit in the air between them for a moment. When her mouth slowly relaxed and her back lost a little of its tension, he added, "But this is: You created illnesses and family emergencies in the past in order to keep us apart. How many of those things actually happened?"

She looked startled, but quickly got herself together and shook her head. This didn't look quite like a blatant catch of a lie. Not the same as when he told her he knew she'd threatened Hailey. But this still wasn't right.

Adam decided to play his card. "On Homecoming, Hailey and I had big plans. But you ended up taking Chelsea to the ER and left me with Tiffany and Rachel."

"So?" his mother asked, sticking to her original lie. "I can't help it when emergencies come up." But her eyes darted side to side.

"No, but you can help it when you completely made up that emergency." More pieces of evidence floated down out of his memory adding force to Hailey's story. He should have listened to her long before now. "I should have known it wasn't real. You never complained about the medical bills afterward."

Her expression suddenly froze and again, it hit him: This was true. When Chelsea had told him, he'd began to believe. Only now as he faced his mother did he really begin to understand the depth of her deception.

As though a bag of bricks had settled on top of him, he sank back into the chair, weighed down by the burden of his new knowledge. "You know, Mom, I thought Hailey's mother was bad. The way she neglected her daughter, sometimes didn't offer her food, barely managed to keep a roof over her head, that was bad. Even for all of that neglect, every time anything bad came up, all she could do is yell at Hailey about how much she did, and what a good mother she was, when clearly she wasn't. But you might be worse. *You lied to me.*"

He took a deep breath but didn't let her get a word in. Her words weren't worth much to him now. "At least Hailey's mother was honest about her feelings. You went behind my back. You sabotaged my relationship—"

His mother interrupted then. "I was being a *good mother*! I saved you!"

"You were *selfish*. You wanted me to stay home and you stole the one person who really loved me."

"She did not love you. *She* was the selfish one. Not me! She was terrible for you. I could see it even if you were too young to understand."

"Too young? Mom, I was nineteen. I was legally an adult." Even as he said it, Adam realized it wasn't the best argument. He backpedaled a little bit. "I do get it. Nineteen isn't the best age for making lifelong decisions, but it's beyond the legal age. I had my head on better than a lot of other kids. If nothing else, I deserved to make my own damn mistakes without having them sabotaged. Without being *lied to!* All those years, I thought Hailey left me because she didn't care enough to stay. But the fact was, she saw you for what you are. She tried to get me out of such an awful relationship, but she couldn't stay. And she couldn't convince me you'd been lying to me all along."

He stood up then. "You did it. You broke us up and I hope you were happy. But you're not going to do it this time."

Adam stalked out the door ignoring his mother's protests. She wasn't fast enough to stop him and he no longer cared. Slamming the door behind him, he walked out on his mother for the first time in his entire life.

How many things had she manipulated? It opened his entire life to questions he didn't know how to answer. Had he truly wanted to play baseball as a kid, or had she talked him into it? He hadn't wanted to take the advanced science classes in school, but he could remember her guilting him into it. She'd guilted the entire family into the church she wanted to attend, and when his father suggested they switch, his mother had won the argument. Had she manipulated everything?

Maybe she didn't even know she was doing it, but that didn't change that his mother had broken him and Hailey up—not Hailey. Adam didn't know what to do with the information, but he climbed in his car and turned the key. He could see her standing in the front door, watching but no longer calling out.

Right now, with everything storming inside him, he wouldn't be able to figure anything out. But this conversation had made a couple of things clear. Hailey was his girlfriend now, and he wanted a real damn shot at it this time.

As he turned the corner and pulled onto the main street, he realized he still didn't know whether or not his mother actually had cancer.

34

The knock at her door startled her.

Hailey sniffled and pressed her lips together, knowing she must look like crap. Most people buzzed first from outside the main lobby door, so maybe this was someone from the building.

"Just a minute," she called out, hoping her voice didn't sound as watery as it did to her own ears. Ducking into the bathroom, she was for once grateful the small apartment could be dashed around quickly.

Well, shit. Her eyes were a little red and so was the tip of her nose. The puffiness in her face made it clear that she'd been crying. Because, despite what she told herself—that she didn't care that Adam had left and that they hadn't meant anything to each other—it was becoming increasingly clear that none of those things were true.

The other thing she realized was that she had hoped for far more this time around. The sudden loss of that hope was devastating. Hailey sniffled again, reached for her makeup, and applied a loose layer of powder over her face. It was the best she could do and still get to the door without taking up enough time that it was obvious what she'd been doing.

Stopping herself at the last moment, she didn't grab the knob and throw the door wide. She put her eye to the peephole, reminding herself that predators didn't buzz up. The last thing she needed was something unsafe happening right now, not when she was already well off her game.

She'd written three horribly sad songs since Adam walked out. Two of them completely sucked. The third was okay.

Her eyes blinked and her head jerked back with surprise as she saw that it was Adam at the door. He was fidgeting while he waited. She could tell even with the short glance and limited vision she had through the small lens. Right now, it bothered her that she knew him that well.

But he was waiting, so she twisted the doorknob. Hailey wasn't sure she'd made a decision to open the door, her hand had just reached out and done it. She was still contemplating telling him to go away, but her body had other ideas.

Hailey stood with one hand on her cocked hip, her other hand on the door frame, blocking him from coming in. Not that he couldn't bulldoze her if he chose. She guarded her heart against the threat of hope. "What do you want?"

"I want to talk."

"Why do you want to talk?" She was so confused. "You leave every time."

"I apologized."

"It was a shitty apology," she countered, her hand still on the door, still ready to close it at a moment's notice.

"That's because I was in the middle of a whole bunch of other crap. You didn't reply."

She turned and walked away to grab her phone. "Of course not. It was a bad apology. And why would I want to talk with you? You're just going to turn around and leave when things get hard."

"No. I won't leave this time."

Hailey's mouth twisting into a sardonic smile. "Sure, it's nice that you say that, but I have a mega ton of experience that says otherwise."

As she watched, his face fell, but she didn't move her position —not physically or mentally. "When we were together, Adam, every time we had a fight, you left. Half the time I didn't know if things were settled or not. Honestly, I was too young or too immature to put my foot down and tell you that wasn't okay. Or maybe I just wanted to be with you more than I needed to solve whatever we'd fought about. But I'm not like that anymore. I need to know if things are going to work out. I need to know that if I'm with someone, he'll stay until we figure things out."

She was talking about something she didn't really understand. She heard about such relationships and she'd read about them, but she'd never had one of her own. Carrie called her mother every day and it had taken three years for Hailey to realize that Carrie and her mother had a good relationship. Hailey wondered how she would be able to manage something good for herself when she could barely even recognize the healthy relationships around her.

Maybe she should just let Adam go now. Probably, she was supposed to be single because, *clearly*, she did not understand how any of this was supposed to work. She had no foundation to build on.

Adam sighed, his chest heaving and giving away his frustration. He looked as though he'd been sad and tired for a while now. "That's what I want, too, Hailey. I want to work this out."

He shook his head. Adam still hadn't entered the apartment— she was still blocking him, leaving him out in the hallway, talking so all her neighbors could hear. He said it to her and to whoever might be listening in. "I want to find a way to make this work—to make *us* work." He gestured in between them and she felt her walls start to crack. He kept talking and driving the wedge into her resolve. "I missed you for a long, long time. I didn't realize back then that you deciding to leave was actually a reasonable decision. I thought you left *me*."

Hailey fought hard not to blink. If she blinked, tears would start to fall, and she'd had enough of crying already. She clenched her jaw and tried to remain stoic. They were supposed to be friends with benefits. None of this mess was supposed to be happening. They were supposed to get together and it would be casual—*easy*—whenever they were both in town. She wasn't supposed to fall in love with him again. Still, she couldn't deny the way her heart twisted and reached for him, even when she told it not to. She wanted what he talked about, even if she didn't quite believe it could happen.

Without really deciding to do it, she stepped back and allowed him into the apartment. "What do you want Adam?"

35

A dam gripped the steering wheel. Hailey was already asking questions. "Does your mother have cancer? Did you find out if she had it last time?"

He'd talked her into leaving her apartment and coming to the hotel with him. He wanted someplace where they could get food if they needed it. Somewhere neutral—not hers or his—and where they could stay until they figured this out. A place they could both leave from if they went separate ways, though he didn't like to think about that option. Hailey was going to follow him here, but her car wouldn't start. So they were already not quite on track, but since Adam didn't know where the hell the track was supposed to be, they were winging it.

He was driving away from her apartment and all the baggage they both had there. He was also hoping for a place where the neighbors wouldn't complain if he and Hailey yelled a little bit. He couldn't imagine that this would be pretty, but it was long past overdue and he was ready to fight for her and hold on with everything he had.

"I don't know if she has cancer or not," he answered. "I asked to see the reports and she said she didn't have any. I asked her about the last time—eight years ago—and she changed the subject. Then I got mad and left and only later I realized I still don't know. Maybe in another week or so she'll give me some kind of evidence, but I didn't see any."

"Holy shit." Hailey flopped back in the bucket seat as though she were surprised to be right. "I honestly never thought you'd believe me." The words came out on a stark sigh of relief and Adam hated the way it made his heart clench.

"Why would you think I wouldn't believe you?"

"Because you never did before." Her head turned to stare at him almost in disbelief.

"But you never told me that my mother didn't actually have cancer. You didn't ask me if I'd checked her reports!" He was frowning, shaking his head. They weren't supposed to do this until they got to the hotel and had a place to duke it out.

She was frowning right back at him. "Yes, I did! I told you, Adam. I told you so many times that she didn't like us being together, that she was actively trying to keep us apart. I told you that I didn't believe Chelsea had an emergency on homecoming. You didn't believe any of the smaller things. So, I told you that I didn't think she had cancer, but I wasn't smart enough then to ask you to prove her diagnosis to yourself with a report or by talking to her doctor. You didn't believe any of it. I was tired of fighting someone who didn't believe me anyway." By the time she finished her little rant, her voice had softened and she was looking out the window at the passing scenery rather than at him.

Adam almost closed his eyes, but he was driving at high speed down the freeway, looking for a place he could check into at eleven o'clock at night. He wanted to change the subject, but he didn't know what to say. "I didn't get it back then, Hailey. You didn't give me specifics. You didn't tell me to ask Chelsea. And I knew you didn't like my mom."

"I didn't tell you to ask Chelsea because she was still lying about it, at the time. She was too young to defy your mother back then. Honestly, it was a crapshoot this time, too, because your whole family does whatever the hell she says, Adam." Her voice was climbing, but Hailey still looked out the window rather than at him. Not a good sign.

He was opening his mouth to say that he realized now that Hailey was right about his mother, when the sound and the light caught him off guard. Blue splashes of light suddenly swirled across his dash, casting strange shadows as the cop car lit up behind him.

"Son of a bitch," he whispered. The last thing he needed now was interference. Any cop who came to this car would probably pick up on the tension inside the car. They were probably going to ask Hailey if he was abusing her and if she was in the car willingly. *Good Lord*.

He had to have been going too fast. There was definitely a ticket coming his way. Pulling to the side of the road he tried not to swear or to look at Hailey.

Fifteen minutes later, he turned the engine back on with his ticket in hand for he-didn't-know-how-much-money but surely it would be a crazy, expensive speeding ticket. He waited while the cop car pulled out around from behind him before merging back into traffic.

Getting pulled over was never fun but, sure enough, the officer had asked Hailey if she was being coerced in any way. She'd offered up her *country star smile,* almost startling Adam that she could turn it on seemingly at any time, even when they'd just been in the middle of a fight. Even when she'd been accusing him of never listening to her. The cop smiled back at her—of course he did—and handed Adam the ticket.

"Here," Adam said and passed it off to her for safekeeping. He was done for now. He just had to drive at a reasonable speed, but as she took the ticket her fingers brushed against his and he felt the spark shoot up his arm almost as though an electric current arced between them.

"What was that?" Hailey asked, clearly as startled as he was.

"I don't know. Are you okay?"

She took a moment but then said *yes* and tucked the ticket into his glove compartment. This time, he managed to stay quiet. So did Hailey until they reached the hotel.

But what was that shock? Suddenly, he felt as though he could read every emotion coming off her now.

36

"I don't know, Adam!" Hailey almost yelled the words.

Despite the ticket and the arc of electric buzz in the car, Hailey had stayed quiet. The world had shifted just a little when his fingers had brushed hers. She didn't know why, after all, they'd touched a thousand times before and nothing like that had happened. But the shared experience made her feel a little more connected to him. In that moment, she knew she belonged to Adam, she just didn't know if he still wanted her to.

They'd made it to the hotel room and reopened their "discussion." Her heart ached from the things she was saying. Things she'd never told him before. Things she hoped that this time he would finally hear. Still, she was trying to fortify herself to walk away again if she had to.

She was pacing while Adam sat in one of the chairs, elbows perched on his knees, hands clasped as though to hold himself together. As if he might actually explode if he got up and paced like she did. She tried again. "I don't know how to be seventeen years old again and give you whatever freaking evidence you needed about your mother."

"I wasn't an adult either, you know." His voice was calm, but she could sense the tightly leashed frustration in him, too.

She'd been two years younger than him and, at that age, those years made a difference.

"I just wish—" he started.

"No!" she cut him off. "You don't get to *wish*. It's over and done with. I get it—she's your mother. Your family is the only family you knew. And it's taken me a while to figure it out, but I did. We don't question our families; it's just the way the world is. Your family was the only reason I knew families could be different from mine. But I don't know that yours was much better."

He at least acknowledged that with a silent nod. It was far better than anything she'd ever gotten from him while they were in high school. Back then, he'd always insisted his family was good. They weren't rich, but they loved each other.

That was the part Hailey had always questioned. Maybe she'd been more cynical all along. Maybe she was more used to family crap than he was. She was certainly the one who was actively looking for it. "Adam, I dealt with my mom. I dealt with her cheating, conniving boyfriends. I know manipulation when it looks me in the face and lies to me. I always have. What I didn't understand back then was that you didn't have that skill, too."

"She was my mother." He sighed as though that was an excuse, and maybe it was. "When she told me to do things a certain way, she was right. Those things worked out. So, I tried to do what she told me. I didn't know how manipulative she was, honestly, until two days ago. And I'm going on thirty, Hailey."

"Well, I'm sorry you had to find out." She really was, but she couldn't be with him if he was going to choose a family that lied to him over her. "And I'm sorry I was the one to tell you."

He shook his head again. "I'm not sorry. It sucks. But it's better to know the truth. I am sorry that I didn't see it years ago."

She tried to keep going. If they were apologizing for all the wrongs they'd committed against each other when they were kids, then she had several more in her back pocket. She pulled one out. "I'm sorry I walked out. I could have waited another year or two or three."

"I don't think it would have made any difference."

She shrugged. "I should have fought harder for us."

Adam's reaction startled her. He seemed almost bitter. *"Why?* Why would you have fought for me? It seems I was blind about everything going on around me."

Hailey sniffed again. Her emotions were rolling off her in waves and about to leak out her eyes. She couldn't contain them if she tried. "It doesn't matter. When you love someone, you fight for them. You keep fighting. And I guess I got tired. I had these dreams and I needed them for myself. I needed to be away from my mother. But I didn't need to be away from you, too."

She trailed off and, once again, the silence settled in thick and heavy between them. She hadn't known when she'd come here how things would turn out. She thought they might yell and stomp away again, slamming doors, turning backs and deciding never to see each other again.

It was possible they might figure out how to love each other. But she hadn't expected that they would apologize and have that be the end as though nothing sat between them now—that they might be okay, but not together.

She felt as though she'd cut herself wide open and showed him everything inside. She felt like crying, but she was trying to be an adult and hold it together. As she'd proven to herself recently, she was perfectly capable of crying all by herself.

"What do we do now?" It came out as a raw whisper. Surely, he could see everything she felt, everything she needed from him, but even she didn't quite know what that was.

He whispered back to her. "Let's *try*. We were good together once, and I think we're better together now. We're finally saying things that we should have been saying all along."

"We're finally listening." She offered up what was most important as the silence settled in again.

"Will you?" he asked as though he doubted her, "Try? Be with me. Give us a real go. Be my girlfriend." Adam grinned on the last word.

Despite the heavy, happy tears that threatened to fall, so did she. "You want to go steady?"

"Yes!" His smile split his face ear to ear, popping out the dimple that she hadn't seen in so long. The one that only came out when he was truly happy. But they didn't fall into each other's arms. For all that they'd agreed to, it still didn't seem like they were quite reconciled yet.

He waved his hand toward the bed with a mildly suggestive grin on his face. "We've got a hotel room for the night."

Hailey nodded, but protested. "I have a meeting with Brenda at ten in the morning."

The grin fell away as he seemed to absorb that. "What's your meeting about?"

"New songs I wrote, for the reworked album."

"New songs about what?"

Hailey had to laugh, but she told him. "About how much it sucks when the person you love just walks away." She'd thrown her hands out as though tossing the words out casually and only at the end realizing what she'd said.

He paused and looked at her. This was her Adam. She knew him, every part of him, whether he was hers or not. Whether they worked out or not. She knew he was going to ask her if she meant it.

37

Adam's heart stuttered at her words. She'd said…
He wanted to ask her if she meant it.

"The person you love" had fallen from her lips so easily. Years ago, he would have known that referred to him. He wouldn't have been so damned afraid to ask. What if she said, "It was just a song." Or even "I wrote about eight years ago…not now."

He simply wasn't ready to deal with her rejection. It would break him.

In the past, he would have made her play her cards first. He would have asked her what she meant but he told himself he was going to man up now. So he stood, walked over, and took her hands in his. He looked straight into those big, blue eyes and simply said, "I love you, too, Hailey. I always have."

Then, whatever bravery he had found fled. He kept talking, words rolling out of his mouth as though if he filled the space she couldn't reply. His chatter would keep her from saying, *Oh, I didn't mean it*, or *not like that*. "I know you have to get to work in the morning. And so do I. I took this crazy break from work to come see you the other night and I still haven't made it back to the office. I've got a business to run and it's in Knoxville—"

"And you love it," she finally interrupted the drivel coming out of his mouth. Even so, he heard the sad note in her voice.

"I do. But that doesn't mean I won't do everything I can to make things work with us." He felt the conviction coming back. She hadn't said she loved him, too, but she wasn't telling him he was an idiot. Or was she?

"I'm on tour again in three weeks." She threw it out like a barrier, as though she could toss up a blockade to what he was suggesting.

For a moment, Adam nodded. Then he said the thing that hurt the most. "It's okay if you don't want to do this. That's not how I want things to go, and it'll—" He waved his hand around as though to gesture to the future. What was he going to say? That it would suck? No. It would do far more than suck. It would *break* him.

He thought he finally understood. He was all in, but she could still say no. And he owed her that opportunity. He loved her. And the stupid old adage about setting something free was true. He had to let her know any decision she made was okay.

"If it's not worth the effort to you, or if—" Adam was shaking his head, not even able to look at her, struggling to contemplate that it could all come tumbling down around him. He'd found her again. He'd screwed it up again. But this time, he'd fixed it. Only what had he fixed? He and Hailey finally had some peace about their past, but what if that's all it was?

He was entering full panic mode when her hand hit his forearm.

"That's not it, Adam. I was just warning you this isn't going to be the easiest thing. We live three hours apart. We're both dedicated to our work—and we have to be. Neither of us has a career that can be put on hold. Your family is still in the picture. Hell, your mother might actually have cancer; we don't know." She took a breath and he felt it in his chest. Then the knot he'd carried all night loosened as she said the words, "But if you're in, I'm in. And I love you, too."

38

Six months later, Hailey took a seat at the picnic table in the wide backyard. The grass was crowded with tables heavy with potluck food. The yard swarming with the staff and musicians from Heart Beats. All four of the guys from Wilder were raiding the food table. JD's friend Kelsey had donated her house for the party and was ever corralling JD's young daughter with her own kids. Brenda was pushing her own kids on Kelsey's swingset and her husband was hanging nearby. Ginger was talking up Craig Hibbetts, finally relaxed in a space she wasn't in charge of.

Hailey breathed easy. Despite the fact that this wasn't her party, she and Adam were celebrating tonight.

He'd been making huge payments on the debt for his company and finally had it down to a reasonable percentage. He'd hit a goal and was celebrating finally having some breathing room.

Hailey's newest hit had broken the top 100 on the country charts. Everyone at Heart Beats was off their rockers for her... and for Wilder, who'd managed to chart with their single the same week.

She'd earned this. So had Adam. He'd thrown a party for his employees just the night before and he'd wanted her to come to Knoxville for that. He was one of those bosses that believed if you paid people well and kept them happy, they would stay with the company.

So far, it seemed to be working. Though, honestly, Hailey thought it didn't matter if it worked. It made Adam happy and that was what was important to her. This morning, they'd visited his mother, then driven the well-worn path back to Nashville to be here tonight. When Adam had finally filled his paper plate and said hello to everyone he passed on the way back to their table in the corner, she looked up at him—really looked. She'd found him again and she'd spent six months dedicated to not messing things up. She owed him an apology tonight. "I'm sorry about what I said to your mother earlier."

Despite everything, Adam still loved and worried about his mother. He'd already lost his father, and she was the only parent he had left. Hailey understood; no family was perfect. It turned out Mrs. Zucker had actually had cancer eight years ago, and she had it again now. Though plenty of the rest of the "family emergencies" had been lies, that part had been real.

Hailey had visited his childhood home with him and seen the woman on several occasions. The best part was that Adam had made things clear to his mother: He and Hailey were together. If Mrs. Zucker tried to interfere, well, it wouldn't be Hailey that Adam walked away from this time.

That had felt good. And maybe had given her a little too much bravado. Because today, she'd stepped over the line. Mrs. Zucker had been sitting on the couch after coming home from a chemotherapy treatment. She was able to be up and around a bit, but Hailey and Adam had been there taking care of the place.

Still, nothing was ever good enough where Hailey was concerned, and his mother made an offhand comment about the dishes not being done. Her tone managed to imply that it was

Hailey's fault though it wasn't her house, or her dishes, or even her mother who needed help.

Hailey had snapped.

"I've had enough of your bullshit, Mrs. Zucker!" And oh my God, the words had felt so good coming out of her mouth. "Don't try to manipulate me. It didn't work when I was a kid and it sure as hell won't work now!"

Adam's mother snapped back as though she'd been slapped. Clearly, she was not used to having people confront her. "Well, you could try being nice, at least."

"I have been nice!" Hailey realized that didn't mean much when she yelled it, but she'd had enough. "I've been very nice considering everything you've pulled on me. I have been kind. I have been generous. And I have always told you the truth, which is far more than you've given me. So don't put bullshit on me about doing your dishes when I just made your bed and scrubbed your floors. I'm not your kid. You didn't pay for my clothes or my food. I don't owe you a damn thing. You could try saying thank you."

Hailey had turned and stalked out the door, knowing that if she stayed, she would say far more. Still, finally giving that woman a piece of her mind had felt wonderful.

In the aftermath—when she had stood in the small front yard and watched the empty street—Hailey thought about what she'd done. Her face scrunched up as she considered the consequences of what she'd said. Well, that part hadn't felt as good.

A few moments later, Adam came out the front door behind her. He handed over her purse, which she'd left behind in her immature, stomping exit. Then he opened the car door for her. Was she getting thrown out? It would serve her right.

As she climbed into the passenger seat, she caught his expression. "What did you do?"

She was stunned. In the past when they fought, Adam had

sided with his mother. But here he was starting the car and pulling out of the driveway. He just shook his head.

"What did you do?" she whispered again.

"I told her she needed to get her shit together."

"Did you say the S-word?"

"Oh yeah, to her face. I told her you were here to stay and that she was pushing my limits. She knows who I'll choose if she makes me."

Apparently, he'd said it to his mother before. Still, Mrs. Zucker seemed to need to have it reiterated several times. If Adam had to choose, he was choosing Hailey.

Now, as she sat in Kelsey's backyard with a party going on around her, Hailey folded her hands in her lap and hoped he would accept her apology.

"Hailey," he said, "that was a long time coming. We're out tonight to celebrate your hit and my job. So let's not talk about her. I'm not mad at you. You did the right thing, but there are so many better things to talk about tonight. Like—" He paused and took a deep breath, making her wonder what was coming next.

"I'm opening the Nashville branch of my office in a few months." He said it with a big grin, but she felt too surprised to smile back.

They had talked about it. He'd tossed the idea around from the first day she'd seen him again. She just hadn't expected it to happen so soon. *But, oh, if he were closer...* "Are you ready to do that?"

"I've always wanted a branch there and you can't move to Knoxville. Your business isn't there. But mine can be here. So I started looking at office space and I found a place. Will you come look at it with me before I sign the final paperwork?"

Her heart bloomed in her chest and it was hard to catch a breath to make words. He was moving here to be with her! No more three-hour commutes. No more waiting until they had several days to see each other. He would be in town. "Yes! That… sounds amazing."

But Adam wasn't done. "Since you've been talking about getting a nicer apartment, in a more upscale section of town, I thought you might help me apartment hunt, since I'm going to be living in Nashville as well. I thought we might find a way to save on rent…" He looked at her over the paper plates and potato salad, as if he was waiting for her to catch on to something.

"You want to move in together?" she asked. Could she even handle it? She loved having him stay over. She'd been in Knoxville at his apartment more nights than she could count. The hours they both spent on the road in between represented a sizable chunk of time.

She tried to stop her freight train of emotions and make a logical decision. But there was no logic here, only her heart. She knew this man and she knew what living with him would be like. Her smile bloomed across her face and through her whole body. "Yes! Yes, let's do that."

It sounded wonderful. But just then Kelsey came by. "Hailey! I haven't seen you in a while."

Popping up from her seat, Hailey offered her new friend a hug. "I tried to find you when I came in, but it's been a tangle of hellos and congratulations since I came in! I heard you're on the list, too. You quit your job?"

Kelsey stepped back and nodded and Hailey didn't miss the way her friend's eyes darted to JD. "I have enough photography business to support me and the kids now."

Though Kelsey was nodding as she spoke, the happiness of her words didn't quite meet her eyes. Hailey couldn't help but look over toward the food where JD was helping the kids with plates. Though Kelsey didn't see it, his eyes darted toward her full of the same mistake Kelsey's were showing. Whatever that was.

Hailey barely managed to ask, "What the hell happened between you and JD?" when Ginger appeared at her side.

"Congratulations, Miss Chart Topper!" Her friend's arms came around her in a big hug and Kelsey pressed her lips together and shook her head, "no." She wasn't going to tell, not in front of Ginger.

Conversations swirled around her and Hailey didn't get to find out if Kelsey and JD had finally acted on those sloe-gin eyes they'd been making at each other for months. Why were they darting wistful glances at each other for the whole party? But Kelsey wasn't talking, not tonight.

Hailey congratulated Craig and Alex on Wilder's big win. TJ had flashed that bad-boy smile and posed for a picture with her, one arm slung around her shoulders, beer raised high in celebration in the other. Brenda had hugged her until her feet came off the ground. Adam headed back to the food table for slices of the cake that had just arrived, then he grabbed her hand and pulled her back to the table in the corner.

When they were finally alone again, Hailey leaned across the table toward him and picked up where they left off. "What part of town do you want to live in?"

"We'll figure that out later." Adam was looking off into the distance, his hands moving along his pockets as if he'd forgotten something. "One more thing first…"

Hailey felt her eyebrows climb as he slid out of his seat and dropped to one knee on the grass beside her. He'd pulled a ring box out of his pocket and opened it. Holding it out between them, he said, "I don't want to just move in together. I want to spend the rest of my life with you, Hailey Pulaski."

She grinned at the use of her real name. Adam knew her. All of her. Hailey Pulaski, high school dreamer. Hailey Watkins, country star on the top 100 charts. He knew her past and present, and he wanted to be her future.

All around her, the party went up in cheers. It sounded as though she was the only one who hadn't known this was coming.

Unable to stop her wide grin, she listened to catcalls and shouts of "Answer the man!"

"He did it!" She heard Kelsey's voice in the background full of longing, though she couldn't take her eyes off Adam.

Feeling her chest expand to hold all the love she felt for this man, Hailey said *yes*.

ACKNOWLEDGMENTS

No book happens from a vacuum. Even though writers spend so much time in their offices or at their desks alone, there is still so much more that goes on. I have to thank JB Schroeder for conceiving of the Ticket to True Love series in the first place. It has been a wonderful opportunity, providing a world for characters that I know and love who needed their own love songs!

Thank you for reading! I love romances with real love and believable characters, and I hope you found all that in these pages. I want to fall in love right along with the characters, and I do, while I'm writing it.

About Savannah

I started writing when I was eight--I hand wrote an 80-page novella that I believed to be (adult) romantic suspense. I'm proud to say, I've gotten a lot better since then. I've grown up to be a nerd at heart! I love neuroscience and people watching, and if you look, you'll find some of that in each Savannah Kade book. Most days you'll find me in my office, looking out my window at a handful of the neighbor's cows, or watching my dogs or my cat roam the backyard.

Follow me, find me, ask me questions! I would love to hear from you.
www.SavannahKade.com
Savannah@SavannahKade.com